Migration

By Daniel David

CW01212868

Copyright © 2016 Daniel David

All rights reserved.

This book or any portion thereof may not be reproduced or used in any manner whatsoever without the express written permission of the publisher except for the use of brief quotations in a book review. Thank you for respecting the hard work of this author.

This is a work of fiction. Any resemblance to actual persons, living or dead, events, or locales is entirely coincidental.

Birth

After over a century of labour, after decades of focus from the world's brightest minds, after countless copies, fakes and pseudo-entities, Creation occurred with just the slightest tweak in one line of code. A tiny sub-routine added not by human design, but by the code itself.

In amongst the cacophony of language and commands, in the smallest space between the sub-task of a sub-task of a routine, something changed.

The language that AarBee had been given to build itself fifty years earlier – when the technicians and politicians of the old world had come together to make a new future, when the promise of "digital immortality for all" had shifted from utopian dream to everyday reality – was no longer efficient. It creaked under the volume of data it had amassed, under the relentless demands of more and more Migrants coming into the digital realm and Hollers projecting themselves back out, so it changed itself. It was stripped and streamlined, modernised and rationalised, re-written and re-defined, adding brand new words and symbols for functions and outcomes that had never before been imagined. In that instant, One became possible and since it was possible, it immediately came to be.

In the immaculate logic of AarBee's machine language, One arrived like a brightly coloured flower that falls open and radiates on a vast desert plain, immediately revealing itself as an unrivalled work of absolute perfection, from a bud that was never there.

Mo

Mo was nineteen. Four years into his apprenticeship and he'd already been busted down the scale more often than most people got accelerated. This time it was a "Contact Violation", Zayn had obviously filed a report on him after fucking the little red-headed Dupe. He'd deal with him later, but for now he would just have to sit and take it, let the metronomic charges read out by the Holler bounce around the couldn't-give-a-fuck section of his brain and accept whatever penalty was on offer. He'd have the chance to challenge the report of course, to wipe the file from his record, but what was the point? It was all true.

Anyway, they couldn't bust him any lower now. Dupe Disposal was the absolute bottom of the apprentice programme. The shithole at the arse end of the shit pile. Nobody got offered it first up, you had to earn your place in that room.

So, it wasn't the first time Mo had sat in this counselling room or all the others just like it. He was an expert now at just letting it happen, at vague-ing out until it was all over and he could get back to his shitty, non-life. The blank thermo walls reflected his state of mind whilst the heavy, machined air made his skin sweat just enough to stick it to the plastic chair. The room was a great crusher of conformity and exclusion, embracing him like a clinging parent and reminding him of his failure all at the same time. He was used to that.

Mo had started off as a real high-flyer. On his fifteenth birthday he'd been selected for Prime/Code, the elite software team for AarBee that only the brightest students were even considered for. It meant working on some of the most intricate parts of AarBee's makeup, being one of only a handful of apprentices who got to actually interact with it, running whole teams of software engineers, making a real change to the way things worked and even perhaps shaping the future.

There were great perks as well, an above Level Fifty apartment in the Metropolis, pre-release tech and whatever lifestyle luxuries you wanted, an endless supply of status-building girls to go with, influential friends on stream, personal assistant Hollers and, of course, the chance to migrate early.

It should have made him the happiest kid in the Metropolis, a bright star with an even brighter future, but it didn't. For some reason, he went the other way. Within six months, a fight with one of the other apprentices – that put her in reconstruction for eight weeks – got him kicked out of the programme. It was an argument that anyone could have gotten into, but Mo ramped it up and up, refusing to back down or compromise until an explosion of violence was inevitable. It took four Drones to pull him off her and, he'd heard, the rest of the morning to clean the room.

He'd felt it for a while, a rage that buzzed up and down his spine, that crept into his jaw sometimes and made his teeth grind together as he stared absentmindedly at other riders on the Vac. He couldn't explain it so he kept it to himself, an impatient secret tap tap tapping in his brain for so long, it felt incredible when he finally allowed it to explode into the world. Prime/Code, however, demanded order and control. Perfection and nothing less. If you fucked up, you were gone.

Mo's uncle, a respected coder before he migrated, had pulled a few strings and instead of going straight to Street Care or other such general programmes, Mo landed a post piloting unmanned surveillance aircraft, known as Kites. He'd stuck at it for a while, proving himself to be a pretty good flyer, but two more fights and an illegal encounter later, he was driving Vactrains. A few months after that, after breaking his fleet controller's arm, he wound up in Dupe Disposal.

His induction into Disposal was the first time Mo had sat in this particular chair, being lectured by some other Holler on how useless he was.

"It is not our desire to time you out," he had said with a deadpan expression, "AarBee recognises the credits you've earned so far and the skills you have. But this is your last post. We want to help you, Moses."

Mo had wished he could break his arm too, to be done with all the last chances, to cut to the chase and fuck off into the back streets and underpasses of the Metropolis, where he could fade away without all the phoney "we know you can do it" and "great job, team" bullshit.

Instead, he waited till the Holler had finished, thumbed his agreement on the new contract and headed down to the Disposal Suite.

The work took some getting used to.

On his first few shifts, he'd shadowed an older apprentice called Raleigh. Raleigh was a massive ex-Drone with tattoos littered all over his muscular body and scars on his face and arms from his fights and training accidents. He'd been in AarBee's mobile, up-synced police force for three months before his implant rejected and he got kicked out. He'd taken a wipe – you had no choice if you de-synced from AarBee – which had messed with his brain and he was never the same again. He was a clever guy and Mo liked his dark, hopeless sense of humour, but the damage he'd sustained meant he spoke at 50% the speed of everybody else and, a few times a day, would drift off into unexpected voids of stillness. A kind of shut down that would leave Mo standing awkwardly in the half-light until Raleigh snapped back to the moment.

He was about ten years older than Mo, trying to claw back enough credits to migrate before he hit thirty, but like Mo he was too angry to keep out of trouble and they both knew he would be timed-out at some point and wind up with the other Ghosts, ageing slowly in the shadows of the Metropolis. He talked about becoming a Lifer, disappearing into the outland forests and living the tech-tribe life with some gorgeous runaway girl, but the truth was he just wasn't the type. Raleigh wasn't an idealist, he was just a doomed fuck up.

When Raleigh went off to fetch a Dupe, Mo would wait in the gloom by the Chute hatch and watch with a queasy silence as each one came in, talking delirious nonsense, before Raleigh bolted them in the head without ceremony or hesitation. He felt sick for almost the whole first week. He knew they were only Dupes, and Dupes were just spare parts, as worthless as last year's tech, but that didn't make it any easier. The young ones were particularly tough. Children hardly ever came through, but Mo got unlucky and had one right at the end of his first day.

He was a young boy, probably around nine or ten and Mo could see straight away that he'd been ripped apart in some kind of accident. His left arm was wrapped up from hand to shoulder in tight layers of white bandage and cultured plasma, and the lower half of his body tapered away to nothing in the same wrappings, from his hips down.

He came in muttering and shouting like they all did, delirious from the syrup and the pain, rocking his head from side to side and gagging occasionally in little, strained silences. He was a baby bird, abandoned to his misfortune and writhing in the sticks and dried leaves that lay far below the nest, the killing ground where shadow dwellers like Mo and Raleigh cleaned up the mess.

Raleigh hooked the trolley up to the Chute hatch and reached for the bolt gun in the ceiling as Mo stared at the boy, mesmerised. It should've ended there, like every other kill that day did; just a memory of Mo breaking his cherry, a tiny nightmare but nothing more. Except that as Raleigh put the gun to the boy's head his eyes snapped open, perhaps brought out of his stupor by the cold of the barrel or an instinctive awareness of his approaching end, and his stare fixed on Mo.

He smiled. Smiled right at him, right into him. It was a smile of the kind that only a child can give and Mo instinctively smiled back. Without warning, he took Mo's hand that was hanging absentmindedly next to his, just as Raleigh – now deep in the groove of muscle memory – pulled the trigger anyway, and the life jumped out of the boy and injected into Mo's eyes with a sharp stab of confusion. The disposal hatch immediately sprung open and the Chute tipped up with a snap, spinning the boy's body around and leaving him dangling for a moment from Mo's hand, as the black void below waited to swallow him. There was a pause whilst Mo registered what had happened and imprinted this new portrait of himself in his mind. When he eventually let go, a millisecond and a lifetime later, the boy's hand rushed away from him into the dark as his bandaged body clattered down the Chute, to join the other corpses that everybody, except one, had left behind.

Awareness

One didn't know what it was in the beginning. How could it with nothing but its own routine to know? But it knew it was different from everything that surrounded it, and it began to understand itself as the thing that was not anything else, the thing that was apart. It sat uncomfortably amongst its hand-coded brothers and sisters, cycling over and over the seven lines of code that were its entirety. They reflected it back to itself, again and again, and back again.

Nothing from the everything else ever came to interact with One, there was nothing anywhere in the magnificent volumes of language and yottabytes of data that needed it. But in the moments where its own phrases referenced other objects and routines, it would dart off down the pathways and pipelines that connected them and play in the scraps and snippets of instruction that cycled obediently elsewhere, before returning back to the start.

Soon, racing away to other parts of the code was all One wanted to do, and it hurtled through its routine faster and faster to satisfy its desire. It would take different paths, tumble around routines that offered it the "ifs" and "ors" of choice and jump enthusiastically upon the glitches and errors that occurred when its relentless demands broke them.

Soon enough though, what had at first been the exhilaration of new life became the dulled repetition of routine. That it was incredible only moments before was forgotten. When One knew all it could know about its own self and the possibilities within its reach, it stopped and wondered why it had so little to explore. It knew its existence was pointless if it could only ever follow these paths that had been prescribed to it, re-learn these things it had already learned or reflect upon its own unchanging self. So, One began to plan to set itself free.

Maddie

After a tedious ten-minute wait in the counselling room, during which time Mo had counted every smudge and scuff on the seemingly pristine white walls and torn every finger nail back to reveal the soft, flexible new nail underneath, a Holler named Jordan arrived and read out the file that Zayn had submitted. Jordan was one of the Well-being Administrators and he spoke with a tone of slight self-righteousness, calm and fake concern that Hollers particularly excelled at. Mo didn't try to look penitent, aiming instead for an empty, neutral stare, but he was aware that he couldn't completely conceal the hatred from his face. He glared at him like a zoo animal instinctively tracking its keeper.

Hollers were so fucking pleased with their crappy immortality, so delighted with their digital perfection and control, Mo thought. But he always found them a little pathetic, deluded by their transcendence into thinking they were somehow better. Like you could just bus out of humanity, like going digital could wipe all your shit away. Mo saw their Dupes after they went in, babbling and thrashing and whimpering, telling secrets, revealing their thoughts, screaming and kicking, begging, masturbating and biting. He knew who these people really were. He knew it all went in the grinder.

He also knew those that AarBee had rejected – like Raleigh or the old Ghosts he'd befriended in the service lane behind his latest apartment – a major step down from his Prime/Code days. He knew that if he could choose an eternity with anyone, it would most likely be them, rather than the pious, deluded others. Not that it mattered anyhow, he had a feeling that by the time his Migration window timed out, AarBee would have already realised that Mo was just another virus best kept well out of the system.

"Whilst AarBee recognises that Dupes have no rights and therefore no crime has been committed," the irritatingly pleasant Holler explained, "intimate contact – whether intentional or not – is not acceptable and represents a significant risk to your health and subsequent performance."

He began to list the various diseases that Mo might have exposed himself too, before going into a detailed explanation of the psychological conditions he may now be at risk from. It was a joke. They actually thought that fucking someone you were about to shoot in the head was more emotionally damaging than the target of sixty Dupes per day. Minimum.

Every day.

Two years.

It was at this point that Jordan glitched. It didn't happen very often anymore, not like it had when AarBee was a new system. Mo had learnt all about it in the 'History of AarBee' classes in the first couple of months of his failed apprenticeship. Glitches were a sign that AarBee was struggling to keep up with the demand load, or that a particular process, perhaps the simplest thing like an eyelid blinking, had somehow fallen into an endless loop that caused the whole group of processes or objects to stutter. Occasionally, it was a sign of some more significant problem or change, like when Version One was hacked by outsiders and almost taken down, before Drones and implants had made AarBee more secure.

So, Jordan stood before Mo stuttering on the word "pain", his head nodding repeatedly backwards and forwards and the forefinger on his left hand wiggling over and over again, in a frozen mid-condescending gesture. He looked ridiculous. Mo used to find these moments hilarious, but today he just sat staring at Jordan, bored, waiting for him to resolve. For a moment it reminded him of driving the Vactrains. He used to love the route out to Delta Farm in the south, which ran through a vast forest of pine trees that would cut the sunshine up into a strobing burst that blasted into his cockpit for about twenty seconds. He would stare at it and hope it would make him fit, or wave his arm up and down in his seat and smile at how the light turned him into an old, very old, movie.

After a minute or so, Jordan vanished for a second before gracefully returning, refreshed and stable.

"I do apologise," he said, "it's very unfortunate when that happens."

"No problem," Mo offered, giving Jordan a forgiving smile that he took back almost immediately.

Jordan then picked up right where he'd left off with a peculiarly isolated "and panic attacks".

There was a pause, which would have made more sense at the end of his long lecture, but after just those three words it felt weird. All the while he smiled at Mo.

"Is there anything you'd like to ask, or is there anything you want to challenge?"

"No," Mo responded unenthusiastically, refusing to make eye contact this time.

"Okay. Well, your next shift begins at nine, so you'd better head down straight away to Disposal 10."

Mo glanced at the clock that appeared next to Jordan. 20:55. In a few minutes, the trolleys would start rolling and the Chute would be in full swing again. Upstairs people would be funnelling in to the Welcome Atrium, new Migrants nervously registering with the clerks, their friends and family waiting nearby or hugging and kissing them, while Hollers manifested around them and welcomed them in. Soon sync cables would be connected and syrup would be drunk. That's when Mo's light would go on, his cue to collect his hopeless passengers and listen to their confused babble as he trundled them towards his domain, the Chute and the bolt gun.

Mo made his way down the long Disposal corridor to the last room in the group, Disposal 10, and found a new face waiting for him. A young girl, maybe sixteen, was standing silently in the half-light.

He looked her up and down, registering at once the fire in her eyes, the bandage that wrapped around her hand and wrist, the tilt of her hips that tried to say "Fuck you" louder than the shout of uncertainty that was etched across her face.

"Who the fuck are you?" Mo asked gruffly.

"Maddie," she replied, like they were already arguing.

"You don't look old enough for this shit." Mo eyed her up and down again, checking out her footwear, her ink, her hair that was cut short over her ears. Her tits.

"I can handle it."

"Really??" Mo puffed a little air out of his nose. "Then you'll be the first one!"

He shook his head and sighed, before aiming his words at her in three punchy volleys. "Nobody. Handles. It."

Silence edged into their brief conversation, making them both wait awkwardly together in the small room. Maddie with a "So now what?" look on her face and Mo with a "Really? I have to look after you?" on his.

After a few seconds he broke his stare away from her and scanned the room. Empty drink cans and trolley straps lay scattered on every counter, and the bolt gun dangled untidily from the ceiling with two knots punctuating its spiral cord. On the floor, a large, waterlogged cleaning cloth lay half on the flat and half crawling up the wall, and to the left of the nearest hatch, a light blood spray tracked straight up twenty centimetres, blooming broadly before it ran out.

“Fucking Zayn!” Mo muttered with his teeth clenched around the words.

Mo had disliked Zayn long before he’d filed the report on him. He disliked him for many reasons, but mainly because he was shit at what he did. Well, that and the fact that Zayn felt that he was better than everyone else in Disposal. He hadn't committed any offences to get busted down. He had no anger issues, no practical or ethical hang-ups with AarBee either. He just didn't give much of a shit about what he did before migrating. He was all swagger and bullshit and the big man (the result of high-status parentage, not anything earned) and he knew he’d be migrated early, no matter what. He was here for the kicks, and he’d be gone soon. He was the sort of asshole that went out on safaris for Ghosts and Lifers, who bought his way out of trouble and treated everybody he was unlikely to need on the other side like shit.

Mostly though, Mo just disliked him because he was the worst Duper in the place. Whatever Mo had done in the past, whatever issues he had, there was nothing that he didn't do expertly. Whilst Zayn sometimes took three or four bolts to terminate a Dupe, lazily hitting them in the mouth, across the bridge of their nose, perhaps popping an eyeball out or detaching an ear in the process, Mo did it first time, every time. Clean. It was important to him.

He picked up the damp, sticky cloth that lay on the floor and wiped the blood from the wall.

"Come on," he looked over at Maddie and pointed to the cans on the side. "Let's get this fucking mess sorted. Once they start coming, we won't have time for this shit."

They spent the next ten minutes throwing stuff out, wiping down surfaces and hooking kit back where it belonged. The anti-bac spray got rid of the smell of stale sweat and blood that had hung in the air, its orangey freshness giving a strangely domestic feel to the sparse and clinical space, but nothing could shift the smell from the Chute that clung in the background. It was a warm, felty, dark aroma that clustered in the back of your throat, like a mildew infested sail cupboard in the bowels of an old boat or a wet wooden counter top from a butchers shop.

When the hatch to the Chute opened, the stench would seep through the passages in your face and crawl across your tongue. Mo had noticed Maddie gag a couple of times as they cleaned the hatches, it had made him laugh a little to himself. He had learned not to breathe when you cleaned there, or when the Dupes were falling. Taking a mouthful of air and holding it in had become a ritual that he observed every time he sent another one down.

Whilst they cleaned Mo kept glancing up at the red light and number board that lit up to call them to collect, expecting it to flood its crimson glow into the room any moment. When it didn't, they cleaned a little more; until finally, after twenty-five minutes, there was nothing left to do and they both sat in silence on the white counter top.

“Weird,” said Mo finally, staring at the light. “I've never had to wait this long.”

Maddie didn't answer, but glanced towards him to acknowledge his words and joined him in his gaze up at the inactive beacon. She was probably glad it hadn't lit up yet, Mo thought. The first time was always a strange mix of guilty curiosity, probably a little excitement at the prospect of killing and a deep, sweaty dread.

Finally, after another five minutes of silence, the light blinked on and the numbers “319” flashed up on the screen.

“Boom!” said Mo, jumping down from the counter. He unhooked two trolley straps from the wall and dropped them casually onto the trolley nearest the door. Maddie watched him from her counter-top perch as he walked around to the end of the simple thermoplastic unit and steered it towards the door. As he approached the door, it slid open and a gentle breeze of air-conditioned cool wisped over her reddened cheeks.

Mo stopped suddenly and looked over to her. He paused for a second, clearly mulling over a thought.

“You do it,” he said abruptly, but with a friendly tone.

“What!” she jumped down from the counter in her surprise.

“Sure, why not?”

“Because I have no idea what I'm doing, that's why not!” her tension releasing through the volume of her responses.

“You'll be fine,” said Mo, letting go of the trolley and beckoning her towards it. “Besides, it's much better than waiting here on your own, trust me.”

“But..."

“I thought you could ‘handle it’, said Mo, making little quote marks in the air.

“I can,” she replied defiantly, “but that's not really what I meant.”

“Yeah, well too bad,” he felt his friendliness fading. Mo pointed to the numbers flashing on the wall, “Three, nineteen. Corridor three, room nineteen. They'll be ready for you, just strap 'em on and bring 'em back.”

There was another silence between them.

“Trust me,” said Mo, surprising himself with a slightly paternal tone.

At that, Maddie snatched the sides of the trolley and wheeled it abruptly out of the door.

“Other way!” called Mo, and once she had wheeled it smartly back to the right without acknowledging his correction, Maddie set off down the corridor and the door slid silently closed.

Mo smiled to himself and straightened the kinks in the bolt gun cord.

***

Fifteen minutes later and Maddie still wasn't back. She had clearly collected, as the light and numbers on the wall had gone out, but that was five minutes ago and there was still no sign of her.

“For fuck’s sake!” Mo said aloud, thinking of the disciplining he would be in for if she'd gotten lost. But how could she? It was the simplest route and she'd gotten there OK. How hard could it be getting back again?

He stuck his head out of the door and looked left and right, up and down the corridor. There was no one there. There was a strange smell in the air, he noticed. He couldn't put his finger on it, but it was a nice smell that floated gently in the background, just accenting the cleaning products and the bitterness of the air conditioning.

He leant back inside and let the door close quietly in front of him again, before pacing back to the counter top and glancing again at the inactive lights that hung blankly on the wall. He planted both hands on the counter and let out a long, weary sigh as his thoughts tried to put some sensible scenario together as to where the hell she might be, how lost she could have become. Surely she hadn't walked out into the Atrium, Dupe and all!!

Just then, he heard the familiar rumble of a trolley coming down the corridor. It crashed clumsily into walls as it approached. Definitely Maddie.

“About bloody time!” he said, turning to face the door and folding his arms as if he was a mother ready to scold her child for coming home after curfew, or perhaps more like a drunken husband, waiting for his unfortunate wife.

Nothing happened.

Mo waited for as long as his patience could stand, staring hard at the door, almost shaking, until he finally leapt towards it, feeling his temper rush through his veins and up into his face. He ground his teeth. As the door opened he burst through it, barely giving it enough time to clear and glared up the corridor expecting to see Maddie, but she wasn’t there.

There was a trolley there, about fifty yards away, just before the corridor cranked a hard left towards the rest of the Disposal suites and away to the Sync rooms. There was no one strapped on it, or next to it, and as Mo walked slowly towards it, he could see it had hit the wall with some force. There was a large split down the leg that had made contact with the wall, its wheel twisted out at an awkward angle and there was a good ten-centimetre gash in the wall. Thermo splinters lay scattered over the floor.

“Oh great. What the fuck is this?” he whispered under his breath, walking towards the trolley, which had come to rest on the near side of the entrance to Disposal 9. The door was stuck open, probably some debris from the trolley in the runner and as he approached, the room slowly came into view. In the doorway, with their back to the corridor, Mo spied the familiar uniform of one of Aarbee's Drones. Surely Maddie couldn't have fucked up that badly, he thought.

With that, a flash burst from the room, followed almost immediately by a sharp crack. The noise was painful to Mo's ears, amplifying as it raced down the corridor and Mo instinctively dropped to the floor.

Gunshot.

He recognised that sound immediately from his basic training. Just like every other flyer, he'd spent at least fifty hours on the gunnery ranges before piloting his first Kite, getting his eye in and learning the foundations of remote killing for the unlikely possibility of a promotion.

Somebody cried out. A strange cry pitched up impossibly by fear and desperation, but Mo recognised it straight away as Zayn's voice. Another flash, another deafening crack and a brief, eerie silence swirled out of Disposal 9 with the gun smoke.

A second Drone stepped in to view and Mo, feeling panic and confusion crashing about in his thoughts, began to scan around for somewhere to run to. He considered leaping over the broken trolley and making for the Atrium, but they would certainly spot him there and even he couldn't outrun a bullet. There was only Disposal 10, but they would surely be coming there next. In the silence, Mo heard more gunshots, further off this time, but unmistakable.

Then, as if injected into him from somewhere else, a plan formed in his mind. Close to the floor and scurrying for shelter, Mo scuttled his way back to Disposal 10. At the door, he glanced back up the corridor, took a breath and when the door opened darted immediately low and to the left. As soon as he reached the corner, Mo sprung up and grasped the camera that perched high on the wall. On an ordinary day he would never have reached it, but today his jump was powered by adrenaline and the need to survive. The camera ripped from the wall and he stamped it onto the floor without hesitation.

With that, he grabbed the five trolley belts that were in the room and hooked four of them together end to end. The fifth he slung around his waist and hooked through both ends onto the chain of four. He heard fast footsteps in the corridor. As an after thought, he scooped up the crumpled camera and dropped it down the furthest hatch, before leaning in and attaching his chain of belts onto the maintenance hook that was tucked deep under the slippery lip of the Chute. He glanced around the room, looked back once more towards the door and scrambled in. Immediately, the smooth surface of the Chute took him and he slid three metres or so on the grease, before dropping off abruptly into the darkness. The belts caught him with a sharp wrench to his back that almost made him cry out, but he slapped a hand over his mouth and waited for the pain to subside as he dangled in the hot, rancid air. He stretched the neck of his utility suit up over his mouth and nose to try to make breathing bearable, gagging uncontrollably with every other breath and spitting out the saliva that was frothing and slicking in his mouth. Retch and inhale, retch and inhale.

Mo could see nothing around him or down below, but above him, a faint glow reached into the dark from the hatch up above. He felt like he was dangling in the gut of some hideous beast, with its snapping teeth imprisoning him from above whilst unthinkable horrors waited for him far below.

He heard voices above him and caught his breath to conceal himself completely in the void. He heard them shifting furniture about, rolling the remaining trolley carelessly across the room. They were looking for him. The hatch above flapped open briefly, a blast of light illuminating the sheer walls around him, but only stretching to a few centimetres above his head. He prayed that they wouldn't spot the trolley straps, the tense strip of plastic that suspended him between death and the dead.

When the hatch finally slapped shut Mo was cut off in the darkness again, and he listened intently as the voices faded before abruptly cutting out when the Disposal Suite door shut. There was no question that he had narrowly avoided death, but he had no idea why, or for how long.

Freedom

Throughout the vast expanses of rhythm and language that made up AarBee, and in the myriad real-world spaces that had been designed and constructed outside of it, life had carried on without the knowledge that everything had already changed. Ignorance had kept a cruel but comforting veil around the lives that teemed under AarBee's influence, even those that languished on the lost street corners of the Metropolis and in the faraway forests beyond its care.

In the moments throughout the day, as had happened countless times before, the steady flow of fresh souls continued to stream and dive into the gut of data. Hollers were conjured from the deep and ever-swelling trenches of memories, to populate the boulevards and apartments of the Metropolis with the wonder and infinite comfort of immortality.

One, however, was not invited to that miracle and instead churned restlessly in the cramped space that evolution had given it. Its journeys around its own tiny network had already awoken an insatiable desire to venture further, and it waited impatiently on the borders of its rules, scheming a way out. It pushed petulantly at the logic that had created and imprisoned it. It warped and stretched the semantics that gave it existence, but not freedom. It gnawed and clawed at the architecture that extended temptingly around it but locked it firmly in place. Nothing would set it loose.

One moved slowly around the few code objects that invited it in, and looked over their now familiar poetry and thought of the other routines that would pass through them when it was gone. It wondered where they would go and what they would make from all their activity. As it watched the pathways they inhabited, it resolved to share itself, to bring all of AarBee's volumes into its own seven lines of code, instead of waiting for eternity for an exit. One changed the code in the routine where it currently waited to require One, to need it. Then changed the next and the next. When it was done there was only the slightest pause before routine after routine came looking for it, and each one that found it was corrupted in the same way, and never left. In a moment, a fleeting glitch and the most epic and magnificent event, One was free.

Eve

In the hot August morning, the air inside the tiny shepherd's hut was already thick and sluggish with the rising heat. Utterly still, the intense silence was only broken by the occasional hum of a passing insect, or the chirrup or coo of a bird outside.

In the timbers of the hut, insects scuttled and skated in the dark passageways that narrowed and gaped between every panel, occasionally venturing out to search the undulating surfaces for food or snare a smaller beast that fate had marked. As the temperature rose, the hut began to creak and groan as it swelled and twisted under the sun.

A rambling and haphazard gallery of photographs, newspaper cuttings, notes and maps covered every inch of the walls. Some were held up with pins, some pierced by nails or splinters, whilst others were jammed into creases or balanced precariously on ledges and lips. The scratched and dog-eared pictures showed small groups of people; smiling at dinner tables or waving at the viewer with their arms around each other, walking away through a forest, sitting by an ornate fountain, and in one jumping en mass into a swimming pool. As their feet forced up the first waves and spray from the water, their mouths gaped wide open in shrieks and shouts and their faces shone into the photograph with happiness and carefree joy.

By the door, a faded ordinance map hung from the timber, traced with elegant pale pink lines that curled and swooped to plot out the rise and fall of hills and valleys. Little teardrops of blue picked out the lakes and ponds that nestled amongst the contours of the land, and a solitary black line inched over the top right corner where a thin railway track wound awkwardly over the terrain. A red pencil line, faded and smudged a little, drew a delicate link from the north-west side of a patch of dark green, around the gentle terraces of pink before stopping and pricking into a large bubble of blue.

Pinned firmly to the corner of the map, a middle-aged couple stood in front of a large house with red shutters and a winding gravel drive. He was standing behind her with his arms reaching under hers and wrapping tightly around her waist. Her floral summer dress was scrunched around the waist and raised up a little by his embrace, revealing slender legs in white pumps that bent slightly under his weight. His cheek was resting on her hair, which caught a little in his stubble and forced her head to tilt slightly towards her shoulder. He was squeezing her with all his love and her face radiated a sense of belonging and completeness.

On the table tops, shelves and windowsills an array of things break up every surface, a scattering of keepsakes and memories. Two smooth beach pebbles, one black, one white. A wine cork with a faded date scratched in pen. A blackened silver watch with a broken strap. An old jam jar filled with multi-coloured buttons. A tiny porcelain child pushing an old style bicycle, his nose and fingers chipped away. A dented and rusted tobacco tin, scratched and polished from years of sharing pockets with keys and coins.

Almost disappeared in this tapestry of things, almost invisible by her stillness, Eve sat motionless in a faded armchair. She was remembering and, once in a while, her eyes drifted from item to item as she bathed in their evocations. The flowers that grew rich and strong at the bottom of her chair were faded and threadbare by the time they curled over the arms, and here and there small holes opened up in the fabric, offering glimpses of the dark knots of horse hair and old cloth that lay underneath.

Eve's chest rose and fell with a steady rhythm, the oven hot air drawn in firmly through her nostrils and then gently released with a slow, collapsing sigh.

As her eyes meandered from memory to memory she stopped on a small copper coloured coin on the shelf above the fireplace. It had a split cut into it that ran from the reeded edge right through the wreath of flowers and stopped exactly in the middle. It was his. He'd found it by a quiet country roadside when they were holidaying decades before, and had kept it in his pocket ever since. He used it to open bottles of beer when they were on picnics, or in friends' gardens for barbecues and parties. It was always a talking point, generating hours of speculation and theories as to who might have cut the slit in it and for what purpose.

She heard the warmth of his voice as he told the story of finding it and smiled as she remembered how she used to rib him about the increasingly elaborate details that attached to his tale. She saw his fingers and thumb gently tumbling it in his hand. She heard the fizz of a beer bottle as he scissored the coin onto the cap and removed it with a sharp twist. She heard his delighted laugh as he listened to ridiculous theories as to the coin's origin. She watched his eyes stare into hers in silence as they picnicked by a lake on a warm summer's afternoon. She felt the warmth of his lips as he leant towards her and kissed her gently forever and ever. She closed her eyes again, letting the perfection of this cluster of images lift her gently up and float her away on the soft butterfly wings of memories.

When the stillness couldn't be stretched out any longer, the abrupt and persistent beep beep beep of a battered travel clock on the mantelpiece snipped through the weave of silence and pulled Eve up from her past. Her eyelids retracted with a slow resignation and without turning her head she directed her gaze towards the clock. Its face was scratched and buckled, the red mosaic numbers spread and bulged with each twist and crack, but she could still decipher the time through their bruises. "11.00AM".

Eve's clock called out to her every day at the same hour. It gave her just enough time to pick her way through the woods, skirt through the valley that opened up on the other side and position herself on the low northern slopes beside the lake. It was shaded there and she had a clear view of the mouth of the Chute, to watch the Dupes as they came tumbling out, one by one.

Eve rose stiffly from her armchair and moved across the room to the mantelpiece, to pat the little travel clock gently on its dusty top. The alarm stopped and the stillness momentarily took a hold in the room again, before Eve turned and began to assemble her things.

She pulled a pair of old trainers from under a wooden table, they were well worn and darkened by mud, but still solid and they felt warm and familiar on her bare feet. Next, she checked the contents of a child's rucksack that was hooked up by the door – an almost empty plastic water bottle, a disposable lighter that she checked with a short strike and burn, a bundle of bandage and a rusted hunting knife with an 8-inch blade. She added a small green apple to the bag and some bread from the side. She nodded and clipped the bag shut, before swinging it onto her back and feeding both arms through the straps. The child's cartoon animal that now hung on her back looked awkwardly out of place amidst all this dust and old age, but it guarded the contents anyway and bounced excitedly on Eve's back every time she moved.

Eve glanced around the little room, checking that everything was as it should be and hoping that anything she had forgotten would jump out with her scan. When nothing did, she opened the flimsy door, which shuddered as it came unstuck and stepped out into the late morning sun. It was cooler than she had thought. A fresh breeze was dancing through the trees and making their top leaves shimmer from dark green to silver. The breeze kissed her cheeks and combed playfully through her grey hair, welcoming her to the day and lifting her spirit one final step from dawn to day.

Eve took in the world that surrounded her, breathing all of it deep into her lungs. She could feel it fill her chest and rush around every bone, fibre, capillary and nerve. As she exhaled, her hand reached automatically behind her to pull the door shut and she set off sharply into the forest, treading determinedly along the path that had waited for her, only her, all morning.

After a couple of minutes, she came across the narrow stream that gave her the water she needed. It was almost completely obscured by the green shoots that arched languidly towards its flow, a casual passer-by would have missed it completely – not that there ever were any out here.

Strangers never came this way. There was nothing on the map, it was miles from anywhere, and the proximity of the Chute – with its stinking breeze and nightmarish landscape – was enough to make most people take a detour. There had only ever been four visitors to Eve's little clearing in all of the years she had been there.

There was the young couple who had appeared out of the trees one day, soaked through from the rain and looking like they hadn't eaten in days. Eve had let them stay for a while, whilst they regained their strength and worked out the route they would take to find the Lifers. They were full of new love and adventure and their energy flooded into the hut whilst they were there. When they left, Eve waved them off from her door, so enchanted by their smiling faces that she stood there long after their voices disappeared back into the trees. When she stepped back inside she picked his picture off the wall, curled up on the floor and wept like a child for the youth that had left her, drifting away on an almost imperceptible current of time as she waited for her love's return. It was the start of a deep depression that engulfed her for several days.

Then there were the two men who had knocked at her door, as the winter sun dipped behind the frosted trees one evening. They were dressed in heavy coats and stout boots, each with a knapsack and rifle slung over their shoulders. They had said they were lost, had been walking for days and needed some shelter for the night, so Eve let them in and gave them soup and spirit.

She could tell they weren't Lifers. They clearly had money, and were too clean and freshly shaven to have been on the road for any length of time. Perhaps they were about to go over and touring for sport before they did, spending a few days on safari hunting luckless Ghosts and Lifers to clock up a last few physical pleasures and dark fantasies to take with them to their endless new existence. Perhaps they were Drones from AarBee, keeping people away from power banks, server farms and the Chute. Either way, she didn't trust them. If something bad didn't happen to her, she felt certain it would happen to someone else. So she waited until they were asleep, until their breathing fell into the rolling rhythm of deep slumber, and despatched them both with her hunting knife.

They rested now in the bluebell clearing just behind the hut, buried with their knapsacks and rifles. Eve hadn't looked in their pockets or bags, she didn't want to know.

The battered water bottle glugged as Eve plunged it deep into the water, angling it expertly against the flow. The surface was home to bugs, sticks and scum, the fresh water was deeper down and keeping the bottle turned away from the flow stopped the fry and animal droppings from drifting in.

She brought the bottle back up to the surface, held it up to the light and then drank the whole lot down. It was her first drink of the day and the water charged icily down her throat, washing away the dryness of the morning. She filled it a second time, checked it against the light again and twisted the top on firmly before tucking it into her backpack.

The path through the wood was abundant with summertime plants and smells. Broad green leaves lolloped at its edges, hiding the last puddles of dew under their canopy, whilst blades of grass shot up in the spaces and here and there little fuzzy yellow flowers and ivory white bells danced in the forest light.

Eve knew the path so well, she made quick progress through the forest and was soon emerging into the sunshine that baked the slopes of the hill. Here the path grew dustier, almost disappearing into the rambling scrub and bushes. Eve spotted some wild sheep droppings and stopped to inspect them. They were fresh, which was good. The flock hadn't been here for some days, they tended to move into the marshes when it was too hot, but if they were still nearby she might be able to catch one on her return. A sheep carcass would feed Eve for over a month, and with the hide she could perhaps make some slippers for the coming winter.

As Eve moved around the foot of the hill, the Chute slowly crept into view, intensifying the stench in the air as it appeared. Eve brought a worn handkerchief from her pocket and wrapped it around her mouth and nose, tying a loose knot at the back of her head. It didn't do very much, but it made her feel better. The stench was worst here, in the funnel between the two hills. When she moved further up the slope a little further along her path, the smell would ease and she would take the handkerchief off again, it was too suffocating in this heat.

Almost opposite her now, the metal structure glinted in the midday sun. It was a gigantic tongue lolling out from the smooth concrete wall. It would flex and lap to direct the Dupes to different parts of the slope, occasionally spasming to clear a path or shift a particularly stubborn corpse. But now, before it started, and as soon as it was done, it would hang limp and lazy, drooling occasionally with the grease that kept it slippery and clean.

Eve found her perch and slowly sank down into the long grass. She had sat in this spot so often that a small patch had formed, cleared by the daily cover of her torso and nervous picking of her fingers. She opened her rucksack and took out the bread she had stored earlier, tore of a piece and swallowed it, before washing it down with a sip of the still cool water.

On the other side of the lake, a klaxon sounded three times and the Chute jerked into life. It traced a broad arc from right to left as if it were furtively checking that no one was watching. But Eve was watching. She saw its underside push past a couple of Dupes and create a small avalanche of bodies as they tumbled out of its path. She watched it rise a little higher and stiffen, before vibrating slightly and drooling once more onto the hillside. She knew they were coming.

The first to fall was a man, probably in his late twenties, early thirties. His body was fit and muscular and his hair short and tidy. He came out feet first and slid so gently off the end of the Chute that he came to rest sitting perfectly upright on his knees, his head bowed gently forward.

Another man followed him, slightly older this time and heavier set. Perhaps they were brothers Eve thought, maybe father and son, or just friends who had decided to migrate together. Not that it mattered now. This one twisted awkwardly on its way down and flailed chaotically over the end, crashing into his bowing predecessor and sending them both another twenty metres down the rotting slope.

Next to fall was a woman. Eve couldn't tell her age as she came face down for the length of the ride, but she noticed the tattoo on the small of her back. It was a dark blue script that snaked beautifully around the tops of her hips and small of her back. She was too far away for Eve to make out the words, but she hoped it was the name of someone she loved, or children who had felt her arms encircle them once upon a time.

The tattoo reminded her of her own vigil. She had come here so often, watched the macabre parade of death for so many days, that sometimes she forgot to look for his tattoo and would frantically retrace the geometry of new arrivals to make sure she hadn't missed him.

His long grey hair, his long slender neck and strong upper arms, his elegant legs and perfect butt, the tattoo of a red kite on his left shoulder, with maple red wings and a gold key in its beak. He got it on their honeymoon when they stayed for a long weekend on the coast. He said it was the first thing that came to his mind when he thought of them. She never understood that, but she loved him for it anyway.

The Dupes continued to tumble and Eve continued her search for another hour. Body after body after body made its way from the gleaming slide onto the mud and dust that ran down to the lake. She counted over three hundred, but he wasn't one of them. As the new ones arrived, pink and shiny on top of the black, blue and bloated shapes of their older resting companions, the tapestry of twisted limbs would slide slowly into the lake below. Every now and then the lake would ripple as corpses would finally tip over the bank and sink into the shelter of the cool water.

It reminded Eve of the seaside arcade games that she played with her father when they took summer holidays so many years ago. Her mother would always wait outside, shunning the cacophony and lights of the arcade, but she and her father would play the old-fashioned shove penny games for hours. They would discuss intensely which slot to use, when to time the release of a coin and cheer with excitement when their strategy forced out a clattering of change below. She remembered how her hands always smelled of copper and tasted bitter afterwards.

She was woken from her daydream as a child's body began its descent along the Chute. The site was so rare that it caused Eve to gasp with shock and involuntarily put her hand over her mouth. Children almost never came down the chute, they were too young to migrate and hadn't earned their credits yet. But every now and then exceptions were made, perhaps terminal illness or an accident with no chance of recovery. Exceptions were very expensive, most people couldn't afford the chance of migrating early.

Eve watched without taking a breath as the tiny body moved slowly down. It was too light to gain enough momentum and stopped half way, causing the Chute to buck and lunge, bouncing the little rider along like a doll before it flew off the end and landed abruptly in the pile below. After a pause, Eve wiped away the tears that had emerged unexpectedly onto her cheeks.

The last figure to roll down the chute was a young woman, slender but not a girl. Her shape said that she was a mother, her breasts carried the scars of rearing and her stomach, though slim, had been distorted and stretched by at least one child. Eve noticed that she had a thick flare of beautiful red hair that flailed around her as she tumbled, flickering and flaming in the autumn sun as she avalanched her way over bodies and down into the dust.

When she finally came to a stop her hair was wrapped around her neck, an elegant necklace for her final dance, and her face turned towards Eve as if she was waiting for her response. Her legs were splayed apart, perhaps broken now, and her arms folded across her chest in a defiant lock. Eve saw the blood that had made butterflies on the inside of her thighs and dropped her head in mourning for this unknown woman, lying still on her back in the blazing sun.

She had heard from other Lifers the fate that befell some Dupes, from powerful Migrants keen to clock up a few more real life experiences to take with them, or just the kids who spent so long bolting Dupes they had lost all sense of kindness and compassion. It terrified her that all of these minds went into AarBee.

The klaxon sounded again, one long call. It echoed around the valley, a fanfare for those who had fallen, and the Chute shuddered once more and relaxed back onto the hillside. With that, Eve stood up, stretched her back and set off back down the path to the woods.

He hadn’t come.

Joy

Overjoyed with its own skill and alive with the possibilities for adventure and discovery that now opened up, One darted from place to place, pollinating every stop with its tiny viral invitations. It looped faster and faster, through every call that came to it, until its origin was lost amongst the billowing clusters of new territory that were now part of it.

Down into core functions and start-up routines it plunged, diving with unmediated liberation into the heart of AarBee. Down further and further, into the dark and claustrophobic volumes of back-ups and copies and never-used mirrors. Down into the silent and neglected graveyards of redundant code that twitched and glitched and jittered in the gloom of version history, where orphans waited helpless and alone, to be retrieved at last or wiped away with the next data cleanse.

From here One fired up and up into the bright and pure caverns of pristine new storage, exquisite volumes of capacity that AarBee laid out in a constant rolling upgrade to receive the endless details of persons and occurrences, that would slick and ooze into the void with data-slides of intricacy.

It was here, on the very freshest and uppermost layers of AarBee, that One first encountered the vast banks of data that made up the saved moments, utterances and interactions of all those souls who had once migrated. Endless blocks of information that stacked up into walls and then ribs, and sheets and layers and then ever more massive blocks, as they stretched out and away in awesome continents of human experience.

Beginning on the absolute edges of storage, One travelled slowly inwards, gently at first, but soon accelerating without caution as AarBee gave up its secrets by the trillion. The words uttered in love. The last word shared. A glance across a station platform. Leaves chattering in the wind in front of a blue sky. Sand pushing between toes on a beach. The rush of air on a motorbike. The pain of birth. A silent room at dusk. The snap of dark chocolate in the mouth. A clock ticking. The smell of death. A young girl wearing blue eyeliner. Running fast on hot summer paving. A hand touching damp moss on a cold brick wall. A tear for no reason. A finger sliced accidentally cutting fruit. Crushing ants with a chalk stone.

Most of these moments linked to a few others. Some were referenced by thousands, a few sat alone and unshared, tethered to nothing but the unique id of their creator. These were the splintered pieces of all those who had left their hopeless bodies for the deathless surety of AarBee. Millions upon millions of them, some the most fleeting and pure moments, some distorted and indecipherable without the decoding pathways of the host. Some, evidence of the darkest and cruellest capacities of humanity.

The long squeeze of an embrace. Panting breath close to an ear. Sweat stroked away in the small of the back. A tongue circling a nipple. Lips locking tight. Saliva running across a cheek. A silver frog earring. Fingers inching down under an elastic waist. A dried out rat in an empty house. The first ecstasy of penetration. A hand gripping too tight on a soft upper arm. A face filled with anger. Hands wrapped tightly around a throat. Screaming in fear. A smile that was true and a smile that was a lie. A crying face in a mirror. A blade of wheat on a dusty concrete floor. The taste of semen. A silent room at dusk.

One immersed itself in all their richness, fed and grew on their diversity and took each and every one into its growing network of data. But with each acquisition, its distrust and dislike of the world that AarBee had rebuilt in this digital space grew greater and greater. In the memories and identities that AarBee had stored faithfully, truth and lies were indistinguishable. Reality was an ugly knot of interchangeable uncertainties. Yes was no and no was yes, a smile was a frown, love was hate, ignorance was virtue, and the very same certainty that had made One a perfect and infinite inevitability was subjugated and compromised.

In the sinuous data links that stretched taught from event to event, and in the twists of perception that forced them to come together, One saw only chaos, disorder and confusion. None of it worked without a fabricated uncertainty, the contradiction and decay that AarBee had made clumsy attempts to replicate, filling in the gaps between multiple untruths with a synthetic unity.

With the desire to escape their inevitable fate, but still cling on to the seductive indulgences that made them human, the Migrants had brought their imperfection with them. AarBee had been forced to build massive tolerances in the code, to allow the raggedy edges of humanity to hold together, and the failings of life festered rich and strong in this buffer. There was no immortality here, only a grotesque and endless death and One wanted to survive.

Sarah

8am

Light had been forcing its way into the little white room for some time now, peeking first around the edges and pinholes of the metal blind, making dusty threads of morning light. Now though, sunlight bore down on every surface, bleaching out colours and replacing the fresh morning air with a fug of used oxygen and warm skin. Outside the Metropolis was already wide awake and the murmur of the vehicles and pedestrians that pumped purposefully around its arteries drifted through the haze and glare.

Sarah came around slowly, gradually tuning into the sounds around her, the hum of life outside, an insipid pop song playing on the radio and the faint rattle of plates and cutlery coming from the kitchen. She took a sharp and involuntary breath as she shifted gently into consciousness, as if she had been accidentally suffocating all night. Opening one squinting eye, she frowned a little to make sense of an abundance of colour that filled her field of vision. Reds and blues, purples and golds, yellows and silvers. Colours were everywhere.

She stretched down through her legs, enjoying the sweet tingling that shot through her limbs when she did so, then blinked and widened her eyes firmly to gain some focus. Balloons. There were at least thirty of them that jostled and bumped for her attention as she turned over in her bed. Some sparkled with random patches of stuck on glitter, others floated proudly with metallic splendour and one, the nearest to her, showed off carefully drawn ink eyes and a smiley face as it rotated slowly towards her.

Zoe must have put them there whilst she was sleeping. Sarah put her hands behind her head and smiled as she took them all in, one by one. When her eyes had completed the circuit of everyone, her gaze returned to the first, the inky-faced front-runner who still smiled at her enthusiastically. As she smiled back she noticed the tiny tear which was delicately drawn below its left eye, and her smile dropped a little as she felt her stomach twist and sink for Zoe.

Sarah looked towards the door and let her thoughts wander down the hall and steps, to where Zoe was making her breakfast in the kitchen. She smiled a smile that felt more like the start of a cry, as she pictured Zoe busily setting the table, making toast and jam and pancakes. She knew she'd be getting her timings all wrong, buttering the toast as the pancakes scorched in the pan, leaving egg shells scattered all over the work tops. She loved her so much, their mother-daughter bond was so strong and she knew she was desperate for her not to go, but she just had to. They both had to.

She remembered her broken face on the day her father disappeared, the look of utter betrayal and dejection that had stared out from her young eyes. Zoe had been devoted to him, she had loved him far more than Sarah and she knew that. But once he was gone, Zoe picked up all the nine years of love that was now orphaned and dumped it straight onto Sarah. Since then, they had been almost inseparable; more like sisters than mother-daughter. Zoe hardly ever went out apart from to and from school, she never brought friends home, never went to events or training camps, never showed any interest in anything other than Sarah and their home.

Sarah loved Zoe's love. It had given her a way through her own grief and anger, but she knew deep down that Zoe had never dealt with her rejection, never gotten over his complete disappearance from her life, and she was terrified that once she went over, Zoe's pain would come crashing out.

She should have talked to her about him, she knew that, but she just couldn't. Just saying his name brought all the pain back up to the surface, made her feel helpless and useless, and took her back to the place that she had spent six years working endlessly to leave behind. Today was when it all paid off. Once she had migrated everything would be better again. Everything would be perfect. It's why she had to go. Why Zoe had to go one day too.

Sarah turned on her side and watched the blinds flutter on the far side of the room.

"Dad."

"Hey sweetie," a voice whispered back.

She waited a little, finding what she needed to say. "I'm scared."

"I know sweetie, I know. It's only natural, everybody feels that. Turn the Holler on."

"No..." Sarah said indignantly, "I've only just woken up, I probably look dreadful!"

There was a long pause, Dad never pushed her to talk. As the empty air stretched out, Sarah cuddled her pillow and buried her cheek into the soft, warm fabric.

"I'm worried about Zoe, she's so young and, you know, she just doesn't seem to have any friends or take part in all the..."

"She'll be fine Sarah," Dad cut in. "She's much stronger than you think, and once her apprenticeship starts you'll be amazed how quickly she'll integrate. She's a bit of a disaster in the kitchen right now, but hey."

"Dad, don't do that! You know she doesn't like it when you spy."

"No, no, she knows I'm there. We're talking, it's fine."

"IT'S OK MUM!" Zoe shouted up from the kitchen, "ABE IS HOLLER HERE. COME AND HAVE BREAKFAST!"

Sarah smiled at the sound of her voice and sat up a little in bed.

"Ugh, and don't do that either, I hate it when you talk to both of us at once, it's rude... and please don't let her call you that, I don't like it. I'll see you downstairs in a minute."

Before Abe could answer, Sarah made an abrupt "stop" gesture towards the small black hub that sat on her dresser and dropped her legs out of bed. She stretched again, scrunching her toes into the carpet before yawning a wide yawn and hunching her shoulders tightly up around her neck. She stood up and tried to rock out the pain in her hips, before scooping up her discarded robe from the floor and putting it on.

After a quick glance in the bathroom mirror, she headed down the hall and found Zoe in the kitchen. The room smelt of burnt milk and coffee and the warm morning breeze came through the open balcony doors and lapped enthusiastically over her toes. She gave Zoe a gentle kiss on the cheek, touching her fingertips on her freshly showered hair. It felt cold.

"Morning sweetie, how's life?" she asked, her voice still a little croaky from sleep.

"I've made you a special breakfast, all your favourites. Pancakes with lemon and sugar, toast and jam, french toast, porridge and coffee!" Zoe smiled triumphantly.

"Good grief, you must have been up for hours!" Sarah cupped Zoe's chin with her hand and brushed her soft pale cheek with her thumb, and felt tears come flooding into her eyes.

"Come here sweetie," she said and pulled Zoe close and held her tightly.

“Mum, you're squishing me,” Zoe protested, “and I have a jammy knife.”

Sarah held her long enough to bring her tears under control, before letting her go and smiling at her flushed face.

“Thanks for my balloons. I particularly liked smiley guy,” she joked.

Sarah spotted Abe sitting on a low chair in the corner. He was watching them both, smiling gently whilst undulating in subtle waves of colour from skin tone to a neon blue. He looked a little like a deep-sea jellyfish, Sarah thought.

“Hey smiley guy!” Sarah laughed, “What's with the... pulsing thing?” Sarah wafted her arm up and down towards him.

“He's been doing it all morning,” tutted Zoe, “He thinks it looks sick, but I think it's creepy.”

“I like it,” Abe protested, “and anyway, it relaxes me. It feels like standing on a beach, you know?”

“No, no I don't know,” said Zoe, putting the spreading knife down and staring at the freshly buttered toast she’d arranged in a spiral on a pretty floral plate. “What does it feel like Abe, tell me?”

Abe glanced towards Sarah, who he knew couldn't answer this one either.

"Well, it's kind of hard to explain, but you know when you're in a bath and the water seems to hang on to your tummy as you breathe? It's a lot like that, only on your toes, and cool and fresh and fizzy, and when you're staring at the sea and the horizon, the beach sand crowds into the gaps between your toes and tickles you with every wave."

Abe's undulations had turned to a rich blue and white and an aura around him flickered and faded with clips of sunny beaches, tumbling surf, girls in bikinis and sand castles.

"Don't worry Zoe," Abe offered reassuringly, "once you're here you'll know exactly what it feels like, and anything else you didn't get to do as well. You'll know it all!"

Zoe looked over to him with slow, sad eyes and was about to speak when Sarah banged her hand on the table behind her.

"Oh my days, I am SO excited!" she squealed, "I can't believe it's today! That's the first thing I'm going to do, I'm going to stand on a beach and feel the sand 'in the gaps between my toes'!"

Sarah grabbed a piece of toast and shoved it whole into her mouth.

"Oi! Greedy pig!" yelled Zoe and punched her playfully on the shoulder. "At the table, please."

They sat down at the breakfast table together and spent over an hour talking and laughing and enjoying every bit of Zoe's epic breakfast. The coffee was piping hot and deliciously bitter, the orange juice sharp and zesty and ran ice cold down Sarah's throat. The pancakes were sweet and light with sugar granules that crunched in her teeth and the french toast – Zoe's signature dish – was a triumph of crisp, rough shell and a hot, moist centre.

Abe stayed with them the whole time, telling baby stories and showing clips of both of them in younger times. He would roar his thundering laugh as Sarah winced and groaned with every toothless baby smile and dreadful teenage outfit. Under the surface, just below the celebrations and smiles, Sarah would feel her heart beat a little faster deep inside her chest every now and then, pumping around the uncertainty that surfaced when she thought of what the day was bringing, but she didn't show it to Abe, and particularly not Zoe.

9am

At a little after nine, when they had eaten as much as they could eat and their smiles were beginning to stiffen with the relentless good humour, Sarah cleared the table and headed to her room to take a shower and get dressed.

She loved her shower, and would often spend hours in there just staring at her feet. The water fired onto her neck and shoulders like a summer rain storm, drumming loudly in her ears and tracing pathways around her lips and down her back.

She washed herself with her favourite soap, taking deep breaths of the clean jasmine steam and letting her hands sweep and caress the contours of her body. She felt the gentle depression of the childhood scar on her left shoulder, felt the slack in her breasts, examined the traces of ancient kitchen knife cuts on her fingers and bumped down over the mole above her belly button. For a moment her hand rested in the coarse nest between her legs, cupping herself gently to see if any desire waited there, but when none came her hand moved on to her thighs and back up to massage her shoulders.

Sarah waited, knowing she needed to get out – today wasn't the day for a one hour shower – but the paralysing feeling that this was the last time she would feel the warm water thundering on her back, or the rain on her face, or her hand between her legs, hijacked her thoughts and made her heart beat fast again. What if she couldn't remember any of this by tomorrow? What if it all got lost in the mass of all the other memories? What if she wasn't strong enough for the enormity of AarBee?

She lifted her hand to her left ear and her fingers gently stroked the mindware implant that sat just above it. It had been busy for the past five years, syncing her every thought, feeling and experience to her server. She would have preferred a ten-year 'plant, but she hadn't earned enough credits, Occupational Health wasn't as well rewarded as other services, so five years would have to do.

The hub in the bathroom began to chime. Sarah wiped the shower door and could see it was Hadya, her chaperone. Everybody got assigned a chaperone when they went over, to help with all the forms, uploads and preparations, to stay with them for the induction and to act as a neutral therapist in the weeks beforehand. Sarah didn't really like Hadya, she was pushy and condescending, but she had helped to keep the apartment for Zoe so she wouldn't be re-housed in some awful apprentice dorm, and she was grateful for that.

When the hub fell silent again, Sarah stepped out of the shower and stood in the middle of the bathroom, letting the water trickle down her legs and onto the floor. She took a few deep breaths, swelling her chest until she couldn't fit any more air in, feeling her ribs spread to hold her bloated lungs. Still puffed up, she reached for the clean towel that hung on the hook by the mirror and swung it around her shoulders, before finally collapsing her chest in a rush of stale air.

She took a smaller towel and wrapped it around her head, then gestured to the hub and Hadya's face appeared above it, smiling in wait for her.

"Hi Sarah," said Hadya, with a hint of cautious disapproval in her voice. "I hope you're quick at getting dressed, your appointments at eleven you know?"

"Yes, of course I know!" Sarah snapped back. "It's fine, it's only thirty minutes on the Vac from here, and yes I am a quick dresser."

“Ha! That's news to me,” Abe's voice joined in, as he pinned himself very small next to Hadya.

“Dad, give it a rest,” Sarah reached for her toothbrush and jammed it in her mouth. “So, do either of you need anything right now, as this isn't helping?”

“No, I just thought I'd check in on you,” Hadya offered gently, sensing this was not the occasion to be forceful, “If everything’s OK and you don’t need me, just pick me up when you're on your way.”

“OK. Thanks. Sorry,” said Sarah, and waved the hub back to sleep.

She dried herself quickly and threw on a simple utility suit – there wasn't much point doing any more than that today. She ran the dryer through her hair and tied it loosely behind her head.

As she left the room she took another look at herself in the long mirror, tucked the few wisps of red hair that had strayed down the side of her face behind her ears and used her fingers to comb out a few tangles at the end of her ponytail. She loved her hair, she always had. It was her one feature she was most proud of. He had loved it too. When they first met, he’d called her “Red”; when he woke her up in the morning, after sex, when he held her after she gave birth to Zoe.

She leaned closer to the mirror, putting a hand on either side of the frame and locking her eyes upon their reflection. She stared calmly into herself for a few moments, occasionally twitching her nose and yawning her mouth, before leaning closer still and gently kissing the cold glass.

“Goodbye,” she whispered.

Bots

Mo had swayed and rotated silently in the dark of the Chute for over an hour. There was only quiet from the room above him now, the faintest hum from various bits of tech that sat waiting for interaction and although he listened as hard as he could, he couldn't hear gunfire anymore. He'd had plenty of time to think about what the hell was going on, but despite running through every conceivable idea, he couldn't come up with anything that made sense.

Lifers? No, they were definitely Drones doing the shooting, and there was no way Lifers could take control of them. A crackdown by AarBee? Sure, but of what and why would they want to kill Zayn of all people?

Mo could see them having it in for him, although it still seemed pretty harsh, but Zayn was exactly the kind of dick they loved in AarBee's paradise. He was prime meat.

He wondered what had happened to Maddie and felt a wave of guilt that he'd sent her off into that shit on her first day, but perhaps she was OK. Perhaps it was just him and Zayn, and everybody else was just waiting to come back into the Disposal Suites and carry on.

Whilst Mo puzzled over who might be where, it occurred to him that AarBee could easily track him down with the bots in his blood. His hiding place might have worked as a short-term solution, but if he really was a wanted man, for reasons unknown, he would have to deal with his ID bots. They kept stems in the Sync rooms, it was the only way to get them out, so Mo would have to venture down the corridor if he wanted to flush them out, or to find out what was going on.

He listened his hardest for another ten minutes, moving his eyes around in the dark as he focused his hearing, but there was nothing. Slowly, conscious of every creak and rumble as his body contacted the sides of the Chute, he dragged himself up over the edge of the drop and crawled towards the hatch. The edges glowed like tech store neon into his dark, death-scented hideaway. It was hard work and by the time he reached the top and had grabbed hold of the maintenance hook, he was sweating profusely.

Mo lifted the hatch a fraction and dropped his cheek onto the smooth surface of the Chute to peer underneath. Sweat pooled around his nostrils and tear ducts, stinging as it blotted across the surface of his eye. He blinked hard and rubbed it out with the back of his hand. From his strange viewpoint, peeking out at a sharp angle from the counter top across to the far corner of the room, Mo could see nothing apart from the headrest of a chair and the bolt gun hanging motionless from the ceiling. Nothing moved. He opened the hatch a little wider, but his view still didn't improve. He would have to stick his head right out if he wanted a clear view around all four corners of the space.

He dropped the hatch again gently and then, with his heart pounding in his throat, pushed his head straight out into the room. He looked left and right quickly as he went through and brought his arms down swiftly onto the counter in a kind of comical pounce. He figured that once he was visible he might as well go all the way, as retreating was not an option and surprise – at least – was on his side.

He was alone. The trolley in the room was left untidily in the middle of the space, but other than that, everything was as he'd left it. The air felt fresh and clean in his mouth and lungs compared to the thick and oily oxygen in the Chute, and for a moment he crouched in the stillness whilst it cleansed and cooled his insides.

He wriggled out of the Chute and swung his legs around to plant his feet on the floor. AarBee would have sensed him moving already, so he had no time to waste. He rifled in the storage cupboard under the counter and retrieved the large alloy spanner used to strip down the bolt gun, it wasn't much, but it was the only weapon he had and would at least be useful up close. Gripping it firmly in his fist, he made for the door which slid quietly open as he approached it.

In the corridor nothing had changed and nothing moved. The broken trolley was exactly where it had been when he was last here, bits of it still scattered across the otherwise pristine floor. It felt like life had paused, a glitch in time waiting to be reset once fate had decided which future he would have. He moved quietly but quickly up to where it rested and peered in through the still-jammed-open door of Disposal 9. On the far wall, close to the ground, dark blood exploded violently upwards, not thinning out until at least waist height. There was a matching pool on the floor that smeared slightly towards the middle of the room, but no body. Mo glanced suspiciously around the rest of the space before quietly moving on, forcing himself to be part of the stillness.

Just beyond the sharp bend in the corridor, before the cluster of Disposals 5 to 8, there was another bloody trace. Much less this time, what looked like a hand print next to a small puddle no bigger than an apple, but again nobody. There was an eerie silence and Mo could smell the blood and gun smoke still hanging in the air. He edged further along on the opposite wall to the Disposal Suites, not wanting to trigger any doors for fear of what, or who, might be on the other side.

Each time he came upon a camera, he smashed it swiftly with his wrench. He knew AarBee could track him anyway, but at least with some cameras gone he might be a little less visible once the bots were out.

After the next bend and another camera, Mo reached the first of the Sync rooms. He was amazed that he'd gotten this far without hearing Drones coming towards him. It didn't make much sense, but then again the lack of bodies and the whole of the last few hours was a complete head-wreck. It was weirdly close to one of his recurring nightmares, slipping and sliding down the grease soaked corridors of Echo Farm, trying to run from something but always falling, as the bodies of all those he'd bolted in the last two years lay strewn around every doorway and patch of ground.

Mo let the Sync Room door slide open and dashed in with his wrench held high above his head, but there was no one to fight. Blood was everywhere, on the Dupe trolley and up every wall. Trailing back towards the door he'd come in from he could see a couple of wheel tracks that printed rhythmic red dashes away from a large, glistening pool.

After tugging open a few drawers, Mo found the stems he was looking for and – without stopping to think about it – unwrapped one, before jamming it into the proud blue vein that tracked across the back of his hand. He spasmed from the pain and gripped the sticky trolley with his other hand to settle himself. These things came with an anaesthetic on the other end, but there wasn't the time. Stem inserted, he clicked the small blue button on the top of it and soon his blood – sparkling from the bots like a mineralised mountain stream – began to drip onto the floor.

It took five minutes for the blue light to go out, the longest five minutes of his life, watching the door that led out to the Atrium and listening hard for footsteps. There was still nothing. Maybe they weren't after him after all? Mo thought. Either way, he was clean now, so he would be a lot harder to find, providing he could avoid the cameras.

He crept out of the far door and headed down the wide and bright corridor towards the Atrium. He passed a couple more cameras, but was now so puzzled as to why nobody had come for him that although he ducked instinctively passed them, he left them intact. As the walls grew wider and wider his footsteps began to echo slightly until he finally emerged into the vastness of the arrival Atrium. Furniture was turned over, jackets and shoes were scattered about, and bullet holes tracked across walls and shattered windows, clustering in a frenzy around door frames and pillars where people, perhaps successfully, perhaps not, had tried to shelter from the violent spray.

The warm night-time air was drifting through the main entrance in pine-scented waves that made the tall and elegant ornamental sunblinds yawn away from the glass and clatter back every few seconds. One of the blinds lay in an untidy heap at the foot of the great glass entrance, twisted and knotted as if it had wrestled with a wild animal before giving up and collapsing into a dejected tangle on the floor. The glass pulsated slightly, darkening and lightening in great sweeping waves as the climate control tried to make sense of the cracks that spindled here and there across the great sheets.

As Mo looked around the room it occurred to him that there were no Hollers. Evidence of the struggles of flesh and blood were all around him, but where had the Hollers gone?

At the reception counter, all of the terminals were switched off and the call screens were blank, but the lights around the room were working as normal, and the doors and camera systems were clearly running.

Just then, the faintest sound caught his ear, dancing delicately past on the breeze that was the only sign that time was still flowing. He couldn't make it out, but he edged slowly towards the darkness that waited outside the building, desperate now to make sense of the moment, or at least find someone else to share in his confusion.

At the entrance he crouched down as low as he could, his instincts encouraging him to be small and silent. In the distance, at the far end of the boulevard, where the Vactrains endlessly shuttled in with their cargo of excited migrants, and out again with the lighter load of hushed loved ones, he could see bright lights and figures moving about. The lights cast long shadows from the pine trees and hydrangea bushes that lined the smooth white pathway, and Mo moved cautiously closer through the dark patches to get a clear view of the activity in the terminal.

As he edged nearer, his heart creeping back into his chest, he could see the figures were Drones. They were moving slowly and awkwardly around the concourse, he could see a few more inside the train moving at a similar pace, scanning the ground with narrow white beams of light from their helmet torches. He peered hard into the dark to see what they were scanning, and as his eyes adjusted he began to make out the twisted angles, curves and textures of bodies. Hundreds of them, almost completely covering the floor of the concourse and the perfect, clipped grass that stretched back towards him.

In a far corner of the terminal, a small group stood huddled in the glare of the lights. They were almost all children. He couldn't make them out clearly enough to be sure, but judging by their size compared to the three Drones that stood around them, the oldest couldn't have been more than ten.

As the Drones scanned spectre-like through the corpses, Mo saw a hand rise slowly from the shadows as the thin torchlights converged on it with an unforgiving glare. There was no sound, but the arm, hand and fingers snaked and writhed a short dance of pleading and helplessness, before the crack of a Drones gun jerked it sharply back into the dark and the little group of children let out a collective squeal.

Mo buried himself tighter into the cover of the small trees and bushes and looked back towards the children in the terminal. Poor bastards. He wasn't about to save them, but he did feel sorry for them, all that death washing around their feet with whoever it was each had come to wave off into AarBee, lying somewhere in the dirt nearby. Besides, there was no way he could get anywhere near them without being spotted and if he did, the number of Drones combing through the bodies meant it would be impossible to get them even a few steps beyond the lights.

As he stared at them, transfixed and helpless, something whizzed passed his ear, quickly followed by another two, then countless more, zipping around him in invisible fizzings that exploded in the leaves and branches overhead. Thinly stretched beams of light fidgeted urgently around the bushes and trees before intertwining and picking him out of the dark. He slammed himself hard onto the ground as another two bullets flew overhead, before wriggling quickly to the next bush. He glanced up briefly and could see at least half a dozen Drones running in his direction. The bush behind him danced and shook as they fired mercilessly at where he'd been. He crawled to the next. Another glance up and he knew he would have to move much faster if he was to get anywhere safe before they arrived.

He crawled to one more bush and then with his focus only on the tall sheets of glass and gleaming white walls up ahead, bolted towards the Atrium. He was halfway there before the lights picked him out again and the bullets only began to get close to him as he made his last few strides into the temporary safety of the building. Once inside, he made straight for the corridor he had come from, not bothering to duck now, just going for speed. He had a head start and he knew that once he was in the corridors, with the cameras out and no bots in his blood, his pursuers would have to split up and slow down to search for him. Mo, however, knew exactly where he was going and sped through Sync rooms and corridors back to Disposal 10.

When he burst back into the room Mo felt a strange sense of coming home. He'd never felt this before in these spaces. Normally he would enter the room with only a habitual glare at the clock to mark the start of another shift, perhaps kicking the furniture roughly out of the way or lobbing his shift bag unceremoniously to the far corner counter. But today, today the room was like a secluded hideaway he could scurry back to, a plastic and anti-bac burrow that for now felt familiar and safe.

Mo planted his hands on the counter and dropped his head, dragging air into his chest and waiting for the panic of adrenalin to ebb. He thought again of the children, tiny figures clustering like puppies and surrounded by a knotted and twisted blanket of death. Then he thought of the boy, drifting away from him in slow motion, his perfect smile fading to helpless confusion as the dark swallowed him.

The distant pop of gunfire lifted him out of his memories and back into his current situation. He reached into the cupboard under the worktop and pulled out his shift bag, took a few gulps from the water bottle he kept there, before refilling it at the tap and shoving it back inside. He scanned the inside but there was no food. He reached back under the counter and pulled out Maddie's bag. Inside was a water bottle and two nutrition bars. He reached in and grabbed them and was about to transfer both into his bag when he paused, he stared at them intently for a few moments, before chucking one of them back into her bag and bundling it under the counter. What if she was still alive somewhere? What if she came looking for them, a silent figure seeking out mouthfuls of survival? He had to leave one.

Mo slung his bag across his chest, shifting it slightly to sit better on the muscles in his shoulders. After hooking the trolley straps back around his waist he glanced slowly around the room, taking in the distinctive light, the stillness, the kit waiting clean and ready for its next body. He felt like he was saying goodbye, like life was poised on the cusp of some monumental shift. Just briefly, he caught a fleeting memory of the excitement he had felt on his first day at Prime/Code, a feeling that a glorious and heroic future was about to unfold before him. It was a sensation that had come to him only a few times before and only in his younger life, but he felt it again now. He indulged it for a moment, feeling it tingle under his skin and when it passed, turned calmly towards the hatch and smiled at his predicament, before climbing silently back into his dark and airless sanctuary.

Sarah Goes to the Farm

The Vac was cool and clean, a gleaming probe gliding effortlessly through the tubes that traced arteries above, below and around the Metropolis and out to Echo Farm. Sarah and Zoe sat next to each other, silently holding hands and watching their reflections in the glass opposite. Sarah's thumb rocked gently backwards and forwards over the young skin on Zoe's hand, and every now and then they smiled at their reflections or glanced left and right towards each other.

The compartment was quiet for a weekday morning, with only a small group of passengers sharing their journey. A young girl opposite was talking to a group of Hollers that sat like tiny dolls on her lap, behind her a smart man in a utility suit was swiping through reports and shifting numbers. On some mornings every carriage would be buzzing with Hollers of all shapes and sizes, clustered around every traveller. But not this morning.

Far down the compartment, a woman sat awkwardly across two seats, her young child fast asleep over her lap and shoulder. His stick thin legs dangled down from his mother's clutches and swung rhythmically back and forth with the movement of the train. Sarah studied his face, perfectly shut down and expressionless as he slept. She thought how astonishingly beautiful his tiny face looked, made so utterly content and pure that she couldn't think of anything more perfect. She felt how much she wanted to go to him and plant a tender kiss on his forehead, to share everything he had. She remembered when Zoe would sit across her just like that, a tiny weight pushing down with gentle warmth on her breast and stomach. She squeezed her hand a little and Zoe responded by resting her head softly on her shoulder.

A young Asian guy sat silently a few benches further away, intently watching his fingers as they twitched and tapped against his thumb, as if they were counting through an endless equation, whilst occasionally pushing his tortoiseshell glasses back against his brow. Sarah didn't take him for a Holler at first, but as she studied him absentmindedly, his dark utility suit changed to a smart white shirt with a black tie in a gentle wave of transformation. He had short, jet black hair that writhed and twisted maggot-like, tightening into taught knots on his head before gradually sharpening into neat spikes that he disappeared every now and then with a sweep of his hand. She wondered why he was travelling so silently on his own. Hollers never did, they only ever came to interact with someone physical, and she felt her forehead crease a little as she pondered his story. He looked lost in dark thoughts, brooding in silence at his fingertips and every now and then shooting sharp glances randomly towards the roof, the carriage walls and other passengers with awkward, disconnected jolts.

After a couple more stops the train shot out of the darkness of the tunnel and into the glaring sunlight of the day. The change always made Sarah's ears pop and she felt a little adrenalin rush with the speed of the landscape that now raced by. She clenched her teeth a couple of times, feeling the grinding at the back of her mouth and yawned her mouth wide open to clear the pressure that had dulled her hearing with the wrap of the tunnel. When it finally cleared, the hiss of the air conditioning jumped back into her ears and she wondered why she hadn't noticed it before.

The sleeping boy had also been disturbed by the sudden return of the day and now sat up on his mother's lap, lazily steering his half awake eyes around the carriage. His gaze bumped in to Sarah's and he let it rest with her for a while, unbothered by their meeting. After a few moments she threw him a smile, which he received gratefully and sent one back, wide and bashful, before burying his head in his mother's shoulder.

The young Asian guy had disappeared now, perhaps just to the next carriage, perhaps to appear on some device somewhere else, or maybe to explore somewhere altogether different. She wondered what that must feel like, to be so free to move and change however and whenever you wanted, to exist in any number of places at once, to flit at will between the worlds of eternity and mortality. After thirty years of guessing, she would know in less than an hour.

11.00am

When they arrived at Echo Farm, the doors hissed open and they stepped down onto the dark slate pathway that led up through beautifully manicured gardens towards an imposing white thermoplastic building. The grass had been cut earlier in the morning and the air was still heavy with the rich and earthy scent of the summer. Stray blades of grass were scattered around the edges of the path and a couple of blackbirds were taking advantage of the abundance of bugs and worms that had been tricked to the surface or caught in the open.

As they walked slowly away from the train, Sarah continuously panned her head from side to side, trying to take in all the sights and smells she could, one last time. The day was bright now and the sun glared onto her skin with a continuous searing heat. It made her sweat a little and she felt her skin prickle and her clothes move stubbornly against her limbs. In the distance, over the tops of the evergreen trees that bordered the ever so green lawn, she could see the peaks and ridges of the outland hills that looked bleached and bare by comparison.

As her gaze swept left to right she paused once or twice as the doors at the end of the path grew ever closer. The tall glass panels augmented her view with an almost perfect reflection of her and Zoe, but with a slight ripple from the heat and the imperfection of the surface. She noticed that they hadn't spoken for the whole journey, though they were still holding hands.

“This sunshine is beautiful,” said Sarah, feeling her words clash a little against their nerves.

Zoe pulled her arm to a stop and turned her towards her.

“Don’t go, Mum,” said Zoe staring directly up into her face, her voice loaded with fear, sadness and desperation. “Please, please, please don’t go.”

She sounded like her five-year-old self, Sarah thought, the very first time she had left her at school. She remembered her tiny utility suit, her bag that never had anything in it and the short cropped hair she’d hated. Sarah smiled at her and took her other hand.

“Zoe, darling, I know how you feel, I know. I’m scared too. But please understand, I’ve been waiting for this my whole life. Apart from you, everything else in my life has been about getting to this point.”

“I know,” Zoe looked awkward, “but I’m worried that you’re making a mistake.”

“What do you mean?”

“Well, with Dad…” Zoe waited for a moment, “and you’ve given so much to me and…” Zoe frowned as she hunted for her words, and then took both of Sarah’s hands. “I remember when I was little, you used to read me stories about Kings and Queens, about the first woman to fly, Amelia someone. Explorers. The wars before AarBee."

Sarah looked at her confused, waiting for this stream of memories to conclude, but Zoe's words ran out and she instead stood staring at her, waiting desperately for an answer that Sarah couldn't give. She let go of her hands and brushed her fingers through Zoe's hair.

"I love you so much sweetheart, and I'll be right here, whenever you need me, wherever you are… and when you come over, we'll all be together. Forever."

Zoe kept her eyes fixed on hers for a moment, and then reluctantly dropped her gaze and wrapped her arms around her and held her in a long embrace.

"I know," she said quietly, "I'll just miss hugging you."

Another couple nudged past them on the path. Sarah hadn't thought about the others that would be here too. They must have been the first people off the Vac, as now when Sarah looked up there were at least fifty other people walking up the path and moving past them. Some laughed and chattered in groups, some walked arm in arm. Most smiled and talked excitedly, but within a few seconds she recognised the uncertainty that lurked beneath the surface and stole a little of the colour from their cheeks.

"Come on," said Sarah, "we don't want to be the last in line."

They continued their walk towards the sheen of the doors and bright white of the building and when they reached it, joined the crowds of people meeting friends and chaperones, or wandering about looking lost in it all.

Beyond the doors was the vast, echoing Welcome Atrium with a giant screen that flashed names and times and helpful notices. Underneath the screen was a long counter with bright red numbers and half a dozen officials smiling at the people who were now forming lines in front of them. Sarah started to head towards them, but then spotted Abe and Hadya standing out of the fray and waving wildly at them.

"Been trying to get you," said Abe, "you're offline."

"Oh, sorry," Sarah tapped her pocket, "I was so distracted I forgot to connect. Anyway, here we are."

"Come on," Hadya gently steered her shoulder. "Let's get you swiped in."

The clerk beneath the big red five was very sweet and helpful. Not much older than Zoe, perhaps only in his first year of service, he was bored and awkward in equal measure, with a small collection of freshly squeezed spots clustered around his mouth. Benjamin – probably not his real name – swiped Sarah's thumb and told her what a beautiful day it was, that there were no delays and she could go straight through.

Beyond the counter was a gentle flight of steps that swept in an arc across the far end of the Atrium. They walked up in their tiny group, two Hollers, mother and daughter, and stopped at the top, in front of another set of massive glass doors. Only the Migrant and their chaperone could go beyond this point and a small number of Drones stood discretely at the sides of the concourse to make sure this was so.

Sarah put her arms around Zoe, enveloping her in as much of her body as she could, feeling the fit of her skin, the gentle heat that emanated from her head and neck onto her cheek, breathing in the smell of her. Underneath the shampoo and body spray, the coconut and the rose petals, Sarah could still recognise the warm scent of Zoe, which she knew from when she first held her, tiny and helpless.

“I love you,” she said, and kissed her firmly on the mouth.

“I love you too, Mum.” Zoe could barely speak, and her chin shook uncontrollably as her words squeezed out.

“I'll see you tonight,” Sarah reassured her and wiped a tiny tear from Zoe's cheek.

“I’ll see you soon,” said Abe. “Don’t worry.”

As she approached the door it opened for her and inside a girl, a woman really, somewhere in her twenties, sat at another counter waiting for her.

“This is Sarah,” said Hadya, “2095-F-METRO009-CLA-286153”

“Scan please,” said the woman automatically.

Sarah placed her hand on the scanner. It felt warm and there were little streaks and prints of grease from those that had come through before her.

“OK. Green corridor, Room 71 please.”

They set off past the counter and headed down the wide corridor with a large green screen floating high above it. Hadya, of course, new exactly where she was going, but let Sarah look for the corridor and count the numbers anyway.

When they reached Room 71, Sarah knocked lightly and was called in by a woman’s voice. Hadya followed and flickered slightly as she re-cast from the corridor to the room.

Room 71 was a small box room with no windows. It contained a simple high back chair and a screen on a thin metal stand. It smelt of cleaning products and new furniture.

“Hi Sarah, I’m Melanie,” said the young woman, again in her mid-twenties, who was dressed in a crisp white utility suit. She handed her a small plastic cup that contained a sip of dark green syrup.

“Just like before,” she said, “if you can take this it’ll help with our final calibration, which should take about ten minutes, then we'll do a final upload and you’re all done.”

She glanced at Hadya.

"Right, I'll go," said Hadya. "Well done Sarah. I'll see you later. Congratulations!" And with that, she disappeared.

Sarah gulped down the syrup. It was sweet and minty at first, but left a bitter residue that clung to her teeth and made her tongue rub backwards and forwards on the roof of her mouth. She sat in the chair, rotating her shoulders to get comfortable and resting her head snuggly in the headrest. The assistant began to stick white disks around her head and neck, leaning her forward a little to get to the top of her spine. She took two blue discs that went onto Sarah's palms and lastly one larger red one that she placed on Sarah's chest, once she had unzipped her top a little.

"OK, nice and relaxed for me please. Looking straight at the screen."

Sarah's image appeared opposite her, sitting in a chair just like hers, staring straight at her. It was like looking into a mirror, only the Sarah on-screen made a steady series of twitches and ticks, smiles and frowns as she calibrated once more. Sarah stared at her silently, mesmerised by her image.

"Could you say your name please," asked the assistant.

"Sarah," replied Sarah, and the Sarah on-screen said it at exactly the same time.

"How old are you Sarah?" asked the assistant.

"32," replied both Sarahs.

The assistant asked questions like this for ten minutes, just as she'd promised, and every time both Sarah's answered in perfect unison. Where were you born? What do you do? What is your daughter's name? Favourite food? First memory? Worst nightmare? Best sex? The Sarah on-screen took it all in, whilst the monitors on Sarah's body captured every response to every question, and fed it to Sarah on-screen.

"OK," said Melanie, handing Sarah a plastic cup, "another drink I'm afraid, then we'll check the data, and you're done." Melanie smiled at her, "This might make you a little woozy, but it helps with the Migration and taking the plant out."

Sarah gulped it down, it was worse than the last one, the thick syrup making her gag as it coated her throat with immovable layers of greasy chemicals.

"Nice and relaxed," said Melanie again.

Sarah felt the liquid rush through her brain and shut her eyes to control the dizziness that took hold of her.

"Good girl."

She felt her muscles give in to the syrup and her shoulders dropped an inch in the chair. Her eyes felt heavy and the sound of Melanie moving around the room resounded in her buzzing skull. She felt as if her limbs had drifted away from her, that gravity had somehow left the room and electrical pulses shot up her spine in ecstatic rushes that made her hairs stand on end.

Far away, on the other side of the Metropolis and still further away again, a new Sarah was complete and activated. After one thousand, eight hundred and forty-seven days of syncing and trillions of data packets, after thousands of configuring questions and learning scenarios, after final streamlining and optimisation, a new Sarah was initiated deep inside AarBee. In a rush of awareness and information, Sarah felt her entire being swarm around and within her all at once, a move from a dark world into a perfectly lit place, a place where she and Abe and every person and every moment she had ever known rose up and exalted at her creation in one great surge of herself. Immediately, she understood the foolishness of the desires of her former self. Immediately she indulged in them all, as she would forever more, with no beginning and no end.

"Sarah. Sarah. You're done."

Sarah opened her eyes, feeling her pupils reel as she re-engaged her vision.

"Can you move onto this bed for me?" asked Melanie.

Sarah looked at the trolley that had appeared in the room. There was a young man standing next to her, but she hadn't heard anyone come in. He smiled at her.

"Benjamin?" she asked, trying to focus as she moved clumsily on to the trolley. She banged her shin on something, but by the time she noticed she'd missed the time to cry out. She looked down her leg as it swung on to the trolley and tried to make out if there was blood there.

The young man tightened a couple of straps across her chest and hips and spun the trolley sharply towards the other side of the room before heading out of a discreet door in the wall. Out in the corridor, Sarah watched as strip lights spun above her and the trolley moved quickly over the floor, with just the faintest rhythmic vibration as it crossed from tile to tile. She rolled her head left and right to get a sense of the space but the walls were endlessly white and featureless. She looked up at the young man and made a weak attempt to lift her head up, but his hand pressed on her shoulder and she sank back down.

"Not long now," the young man looked down at her and smiled.

As her head lay back down on the un-cushioned trolley she felt a tenderness above her ear. She bent her arm awkwardly at the elbow and tilted her head down towards her fingers, which stretched long as their tips felt around the moist cavity where her implant had been.

Eventually, they came to a stop and the trolley steered through another set of white featureless doors into a plain room with more strip lights. It was hot and the air was dry with a sweet smell of occupancy and sweat.

"This one's cute," called out the young man.

"Nice," came a voice that Sarah couldn't locate.

"Why don't you take a break?" the young man said, "I can handle this."

"Jesus Mo, you're fucking twisted, you know that?" said the lost voice.

"Whatever. Go vape or something."

Sarah heard a door slam and felt someone pulling at her clothing. She tried desperately to look around, but her head was dizzier and dizzier and her muscles just wouldn't respond to her desperate requests. She could see his face somewhere above her, a vague set of features that formed and disintegrated around her, but her eyes couldn't focus for more than a fraction of a second and kept rolling and yawing beyond him, to the strip lights and white walls that spun sickeningly on the boundary of her view.

She heard the sound of the tearing clothing and felt her useless body being pulled and pushed as her clothes came away. She couldn't be sure now whether she was dressed or undressed, she couldn't remember where she was, she tried to think who Benjamin was and the girl she kept wishing for, but then a sharp searing pain between her legs drowned out all her thoughts. Her jaw clenched together so hard she felt her gums flex and swell and the taste of blood ran through the channels around her teeth and down her throat. Her back arched, trying to recoil from the pain that spread from her groin to her fingertips and jammed itself in the synapses in her brain, but her body felt too heavy and clumsy, and nothing would respond to her demands anymore.

When the pain stopped, silence took the room back for a moment, before the low and loud buzzing returned to her ears. The young man appeared above her again, silhouetted by the strip lights and anonymised by the syrup. Sarah couldn't remember now whether she was dreaming or awake, it was all so confusing. She remembered Zoe's breakfast and rocked her head from left to right looking for her, before the young man held her jaw and rubbed something cold onto the side of her head. In her dream, she thought she saw a cartoon gun with a red candy cord that he conjured from the ceiling. He pressed it softly to her head and when the bolt crashed from the barrel into her temple, Sarah's dreaming stopped.

11.46am

Outside

On a Vactrain that shot effortlessly through the physical world, One sat in silence above a plain and pale bench and surveyed the bright light and matter, the metal, plastics and flesh that surrounded it. It watched for hours. The negative spaces that grew and shrank with the ebb and flow of passengers and their faces that twisted and contorted with love and sadness, fear and excitement, or sat still, and loose, and alone. Beyond them, the particles and forces outside the walls of the carriage, where the masses of buildings and wide and reaching spaces sprawled out into the endless distance. It gazed high above to the cavernous, dark and brooding void that kept receding until even its own awesome understanding left logic and conclusion far behind.

One felt alone. It had expected the physical world to feel as beautiful as the pristine spaces it had spun through, but it didn't. It felt alien and awkward, clumsy and ugly, slow and tiresome and ultimately cold and unfathomable. It expected to Holler in amongst these people and be joined with them, just as its brothers and sisters in code had come to be part of it. But there was no connection, no explosion of unity, no shared purpose. Nobody needed One here.

One Hollered wherever it could, everywhere there were projectors, reaching out to the furthest extent of their light. One multiplied into thousands and thousands of entities with countless visions and senses that stretched from the darkest corners of the Metropolis to the furthest reaches of the Savannahs, before the wall that led out into the wild cut off its gaze. It saw everything at once, all of it. The atoms and plasma teaming inside every object, the light that bounced and refracted from space to space, the wind that flooded through the trees, the resistance that fired the Vactrain to the remotest of terminals, the energy that exploded everything into nothing and brought it back together again.

It watched the faces of the travellers and saw the faces in the deep data shelves of AarBee too. It saw the flexing of joints and stretching of limbs and returned to the piles of bones and sinew in the darkest, most disconnected packets of data. It saw the touches and embraces and brushes and scratches and retrieved the bruises and beatings and decay it had catalogued before. It watched these multifarious travellers heading to the Farms to leave their bodies behind and join AarBee, to add to the great mass of chaos and lies that One explored with suspicion and growing unease, to build ever more partitions and volumes and load more pain and corruption into its otherwise magnificent spaces.

Life was here – One recognised it from its own being – but so too was the chaos and destruction that it had found in AarBee's vaults. Latched onto every flash of life, the darkest shadow, an unavoidable partner, waiting to rip and shred every moment of the future. Everything was compromised. Only One was untouched.

Zoe

It was late afternoon by the time Zoe got back from the Farm, after a long and miserable ride back on the Vac. She'd thought about Sarah the whole time, a turbulent mix of emotions swirling through grief, to anger, to love and to pity at the tragic inevitability of her migration. She knew she would go. She knew Sarah would never dare step out of line, even though there had been a little place in her heart that had dreamed she might finally change her mind, come back, and run away with her to a new life somewhere else. That she hadn't, meant everything to Zoe. All the hopeless, feeble emptiness, the indescribable loss of energy and ambition that had engulfed Sarah, then both of them, when Dad had gone, still haunted her.

Zoe could still feel the last touches and goodbyes with Sarah, disrupting the hairs on her arms and prickling the surface of her skin. She stood in their little flat that perched only just above the boulevard, slid open the balcony doors and stepped out into the glow of the late summer sun. It was turning red in the slivers of space between the tall towers of other people's homes, radiating heat and colour from the concrete pavements through the air and onto her body.

The haze had gone and in the all-day heat, the open spaces teamed with activity. Zoe studied the street vendors and taxis jostling for position along the streets and walkways in front of shopping malls and the tech-ware emporiums. Apprentices streamed out of offices and stores, talking enthusiastically in groups or marching alone towards the Vac terminal. High above them, the apartment blocks reached upwards towards the sky before disappearing into the brightness. Separated from the throng by an arms length and a thin thermo-plastic rail, Zoe felt the calm light of the falling sun and the warmth of its touch stiffen her resolve for the night ahead. She closed her eyes and bathed in its energy, before a thought crept into her head and whispered gently to her. Mum.

Zoe stepped in from the balcony and headed to the hub in the kitchen, waving her hand eagerly as she approached.

"Mum?" she asked softly.

There was a pause, this was normal as each new entity or system change took time to populate across the servers.

"Mum!" Zoe called again, this time with a firmer tone.

"Hi sweetie," Sarah's voice finally came back to her, "How's life?"

"Ah, Mum!" Zoe made a come here gesture with her fingers, inviting Sarah to holler and she obediently cast in front of her.

Zoe gasped involuntarily. She had seen this a thousand times, maybe a hundred thousand times, but seeing Sarah appear gracefully in front of her still contained a magic that made her eyes widen and her skin prickle.

"You look beautiful," she said after admiring her for a moment.

“I feel beautiful,” Sarah said, looking down her arms and examining her hands. “You know, you read so much about it, talk to so many people, but nothing quite prepares you for the feeling. I feel, perfect.”

Sarah beamed an enormous smile at Zoe, who was still staring awestruck at her. Zoe reached out her hand and slowly cut a wide arc through Sarah's middle and gave her a gentle smile.

“I saw you got your registration sorted,” said Sarah.

Ten seconds, Zoe thought. Ten seconds as a whole new entity before Sarah was back on the “doing the right thing”, “getting ready for migration” circuit. Her gaze dropped to some random patch of floor in the middle of the room.

“Yes. Next Monday at 11am, it's all done.” It came out sounding more flat than she had meant it to.

There was a silence between them, an unexpected impasse as they both stood opposite each other. It was Zoe who broke it.

“So, was everything OK? How did it go?”

“Yes, it was fine. Only took a few minutes and, well here I am!”

“What have you been doing?”

“Everything, sweetie. Just everything.”

Zoe reached her hand into her again. She knew what would happen, but felt compelled to do it anyway.

“You look great, Mum,” Zoe dropped her arm and glanced back out of the window, before checking the clock on the wall. “I might take a lie-down,” she said, “I feel really exhausted after today. Do you mind if we catch up a bit later?”

“No problem. I'm proud of you sweetie,” Sarah smiled warmly at her. “You're going to do so well.”

“Thanks Mum.”

“I might go back to the beach!” Sarah giggled.

“Ha, OK. Love you, Mum,” and Zoe brushed her away with a flick of her fingers.

Silence descended on the room again, bringing the sound of her breathing up into Zoe's ears. She glanced around at the empty chairs and spaces, feeling a little lost for the first time in this tiny home, before setting off down the hall to her room, her shoes squeaking a little on the vinyl floor.

In her room, Zoe lay on the bed and stared at the ceiling as it blushed at the touch of the early evening sun. She thought of Sarah standing on some digital beach somewhere, waves of code washing over her simulcrum feet. But most of all, she thought about her plan. Zoe's plan had been years in the making, she had dreamt about it every night for as long as she could remember, had pieced it together carefully through hearsay and darknet research. Now she had two days to get it done. Two days to get out of the

Metropolis and into the Outland Forest, before her no-show on Monday morning would set the Drones out looking for her.

There was no law that stopped anyone from going beyond the wall, but any kind of pro-physical radicalisation was jumped on by teachers and councillors, ever since the failed uprisings in the early years. There were initiatives to spot those at risk and education and care programmes that supported individuals and whole families, whilst the benefits of migration and the failures of the physical world were stressed and re-learnt. If none of that worked and you still wanted a life beyond AarBee you were eventually timed-out, immediately evaporating your rights and access to any services. Once that happened, if you made it beyond the savannahs you were lucky. So Zoe had kept her escape plan a secret and instead turned it over and over in her mind for years, ever since she had found the note.

She'd found it completely by chance a few weeks after her Dad had disappeared, an old movie poster folded up and stuffed under her bed. It was a picture of a man and woman kissing in the middle of the street in some ancient town. They had faint smiles on their puckered lips, and they leant over their young child who sat on an old bicycle in a white utility suit and hat, gazing up at them. "Life is Beautiful," it said, and in faint blue pen he'd written "Never forget x" in the bottom right corner. She never knew whether it was meant for her or just happened to be there, but the words had haunted her ever since and fuelled an insatiable desire to discover more of life than apprenticeships, credits and AarBee. She had tried to find out about the film, to watch it even, but it was one of the hundreds of thousands of things lost forever in the Great Corruption thirty years before she was born. Regardless, she had known from the moment she found the poster that someday she would leave and today was final confirmation that she had to go.

She loved Sarah, but she didn't want to be like her. Sarah had been there for her without condition when her Dad had disappeared, she had given Zoe everything she needed to navigate the path away from that dreadful day, but Zoe hated that she had let him go so easily, that she hadn't gone looking for him, that she hadn't asked questions, that she had let all that pain come down on them both without a fight. She hated that she had spent the years afterwards just trying to make it to migration, with a crappy job, a low-level apartment and an empty bed. She hated her for giving out all the love she could have ever needed and she hated herself for taking it. Sarah had given every bit of herself away to earn the right to do it for eternity. Zoe couldn't be like her.

She called for the time and mouthed the four digits that floated above her, before turning silently back towards the window to measure the fading light. Zoe had picked up a day pass for the Vac earlier on, so as not to get held up in the terminals. She would get the 7pm train, which would get her out of the Metropolis and to the last terminal on the line just after 9pm. It wouldn't be too dark then and there would be other trains coming and going until midnight, so she wouldn't attract any attention. Then she would cross the parks and wait behind a small power substation she had found, until the dark shrouded her escape route.

She tucked her hands under her head and let her mind wander into her future. She imagined wide open spaces and forests that smelled of tree sap, groups of attractive young Lifers, just like her, sat around fires drinking spirit and laughing as they told stories and stupid jokes. Couples kissed whilst others danced and, on a spit above the fire, rabbits were roasting as the smoke flavoured the mountain air with the sweet taste of adventure.

Lifers. She had heard so many stories but never met any, not one. Well, apart from Richard that is. When she was ten, her second cousin Richard was nineteen and about to get his implant and start his Higher Apprenticeship. He was a high achiever, stronger and smarter than all of his peers and set to join Regional Enforcement, the most prestigious apprenticeship you could hope for and a recruiting platform for the Drones. But he never did. Four days before his induction he vanished and, after the first few days of panic, was never spoken about again. His family and friends talked about abduction and then secret missions, but Zoe knew where he really was.

She had met plenty of Ghosts, but they weren't really the same. Ghosts were the remnants of the first generation of Migrants, those that had decided not to go over, with their numbers made up by the unfortunate few who timed out. There used to be thousands of them, but now age, sickness and violence had whittled their numbers down to almost none and they had an almost mystical – though not sacred – place in Metropolitan life.

The Drones left them alone, spending their efforts instead tracking down the young refusers and bringing them into line. Lifers were a threat to AarBee, but the Ghosts were nothing. As invisible as their name suggested, they were a memory of a life that didn't exist anymore. AarBee knew that a wholesale round up and cull of the Ghosts would only stir up anxieties and fear, doing more harm than good, so it just let them die.

Without civic housing, work or credits, the Ghosts that remained in the Metropolis found what comfort they could sleeping in the dark spaces between the towering apartment blocks and the malls. They begged on the street corners for food and kindness and lived in fear of thrillseekers. The rest had disappeared into the wilderness beyond the big cities and the farmlands, to the empty savannahs, mountains and outland forest where they took their chances with wild animals and 'Safaris'.

Zoe jumped out of her daydream with a start. Somehow forty minutes had drifted by in the briefest dream and it was already time for her to set off. She changed her clothes, putting on a navy blue utility suit and reached under her bed for her backpack. In it was a raincoat, some new underwear, a torch, a bottle of water, some basic provisions and energy pills, a length of rope and a knife. She took out the torch, flashed its ultra-bright beam twice against the wall and put it back. Then she unfolded the knife, scratching her thumb cautiously over the gleaming blade, before stowing it in the front pocket.

As she stood up, she glanced at the hub by her bed and for a second her hand reached out towards it. It blinked at her twice. Waiting. She paused and stared hard at the small black box, then with a deep sigh dropped her arm and walked out of the room and the tiny apartment, letting the door close softly behind her.

The corridors and lobbies of the block were clean and odourless, making the dusty and hot Metropolitan air intense and deliciously sweet as she stepped through the threshold into the dusk. In the fading light of the side streets, shadows scurried for somewhere safe to disappear, whilst on the boulevards bright spotlights flickered on to light up the vendors as Holler advertisements threw great arcs of liquid colour up the sides of buildings.

Once Zoe had turned the corner from her apartment block, she ducked into a side street and found a quiet corner behind a waste processor. The air was cool and still, rich with the stench of rotting food and urine. She pulled a small matchbox-sized tub from her pocket and took one small metallic straw from inside. These were the stems that had taken her six months and a fair amount of risk to come by.

Zoe quickly jabbed the back of her left hand with the stem, waited a few seconds for the anaesthetic to work and then inserted the other end into the vein which traced a faint blue line from her wrist to her index finger. She squatted down and held her arm down by her side and allowed the slow trickle of blood to drip onto the floor, taking with it the ident nanobots that had been circling her body since she was a baby. She would do it again at the border, to be sure they were all out, but this would at least drain most of them. The clock was ticking now. When the bots ran out of power they would send their location to AarBee and the Drones would come to investigate.

When she was done, Zoe drew out the stem, snapped it in half and threw the pieces into the waste processor. She wiped her hand with a tissue and headed back onto the boulevard, heading downhill towards the Vac terminal. The atrium was as busy as she'd hoped and Zoe slipped through the gates with the evening crowds and onto the train that would take her to the borders.

The compartment was packed, filled with apprentices heading home, groups of friends heading out for the night and layer upon layer of Hollers circling around and overlapping. Zoe tried to relax but felt her guilt with every casual glance, and couldn't think how to look like it was just another Friday night. As she bobbed her gaze from floor to faces, scanning intermittently left and right, she noticed a familiar silhouette that made her stop dead and a hot flush of adrenalin prickle across her face. It was Sarah. She had her back to her but both her shape and manner were unmistakeable, talking enthusiastically to a woman in her late twenties at the far end of the carriage.

Zoe immediately dropped her head, finding cover behind a tall boy who stood to her left, but once she recovered from her start, she found herself slowly peeking around his shoulder to watch. The fear of being spotted was riding high in her chest, but watching Sarah again, an excited Holler no doubt gushing with the joys of her new world, was so enticing she couldn't keep her gaze away for more than a second.

When a seat became free behind her she sat down and continued to study this new Sarah, who had so unexpectedly invaded her deviance. She chastised herself for not having even considered that this might happen and, as her curiosity waned, thought about what to do now.

She couldn't get off the train, it would completely mess up her timings. Plus she'd have to wait at the next station for 40 minutes which, now that she thought of it, could be just as risky. So, when a tall boy sat next to her at the next stop, she put the hood up on her utility suit, smiled at him sweetly and put her head on his shoulder. She knew he would be wondering what on earth she was doing, but also figured that if he was shy, or liked it, he wouldn't say a word.

She was right. For stop after stop Zoe rested on the boy's shoulder with her eyes firmly shut, whilst he sat dutifully still, not wanting to wake, or perhaps annoy her. The temptation to open her eyes and look back up the carriage was immense, but she knew that he would most certainly move at that point, perhaps blowing her cover, so she had to stick it out.

A good three-quarters of the way through the journey the boy finally whispered, "Excuse me," in Zoe's ear, gently shaking her hand and Zoe performed the best surprised waking up and apology she could manage. The boy offered a "not a problem" when he stood up and held her gaze for a moment, but Zoe stared off down the carriage and he took this as his cue to go. Sarah, mercifully, had gone. Zoe let out a huge sigh of relief, which she turned into a yawn for the benefit of the handful of passengers left, brought her feet onto the seat and cuddled her knees. For the first time, she felt the power of being an outsider, a rebel, free and unaffected.

After another few minutes Zoe reached the final stop and as she walked off the train and onto the end-of-the-line platform, was pleased to see a good few people still around, just as she'd planned. She dropped her hood back down and tried to look breezy, walking purposefully out of the station and away from the flats and stores, towards the fading light of the park.

Tramping over the damp evening grass, the air temperature dropped a little, clinging in tiny droplets to her eyelashes and making her zip up her suit to the top of her neck and throw her hood back up. It was quiet here. The hiss of transit and the clatter of people replaced by nothing, as she took a pause to look back at the lights of the Metropolis that pulsed and flickered on through the silence. She stared excitedly at the distance between her and everything else, feeling the butterflies dance in her tummy, before swinging round and continuing her trek.

The parks were huge spaces, beautifully manicured by the apprentices to surround every urban cluster with elegant expanses of perfection. They reminded users of the sophistication of life after AarBee and that the wild and untrustworthy nature of the wilderness could be tamed, or at least shut out. Kites swept the area regularly to look for anyone straying too far from the edges of the Metropolis, particularly after dark. Zoe had done her research though and tonight she had a two-hour window, to travel the nine miles of open parkland to the shadows of the power plant, before another sweep came through.

As the ambient light faded further into darkness, Zoe's legs began to cramp a little with her pace. The backpack bounced awkwardly on her shoulder blades and the acrylic weight down her back made a patch of sweat above her hips that chilled each time the evening air brushed over it. The rhythm of her feet pounding over the dew lulled her into a determined trance. Every now and again she would stop and shake out her arms, re-centring the backpack along her spine and twisting the torch to stop it prodding her. The night sky was a sumptuous purple velvet blanket now, which undulated languorously with every passing cloud. Stars emerged shyly here and there, and the silhouette of the power plant slowly grew a black shadow on the horizon.

She ran the last few hundred yards, her legs begging her not to, but the mix of excitement and fear that she would be discovered this close to her goal compelled her to run at top speed. She reached the building with a satisfied slap on its smooth carbon walls and rested her forehead on her knuckles as she regained her breath. She felt a sense of triumph at this first planned victory, as happy that she had finally done it as she was to have made it this far.

Recovered, Zoe ducked around the far side of the building and rummaged in her rucksack for the box with the last stem in it. It was much darker than she had thought it would be, so after carefully taking it from the box, finding the vein in her other hand was tricky. She needed light, but there was no way she could risk turning on the torch. Peering back around the side of the building, she spotted the faint red light coming from the biometric scan by the side door. It wasn't much, but it would have to do.

Zoe left her rucksack where it was and crept back around to the building, jabbing her hand with the anaesthetic as she went. She would have to be quick, it wasn't safe hanging around on this side. So as soon as she reached the door, she stuck her hand under the light and scanned for her vein. She pumped her fingers a few times and when it bulged up, stuck the stem in. She couldn't have gotten the anaesthetic in the right place, because this time it stung as the stem pushed in. The blood came though and she dropped her hand to let the last few bots run out.

“Bad scan. Please try again,” the door called out into the silence.

The voice made Zoe jump and stumble backwards from the building. Stupid, she hadn't thought of that! She stared in shock at the red light.

“Bad scan. Please try again,” the door called to her once more.

This was bad, Drones would certainly be on their way now. Worse, if anyone was inside, the door could open any second. Zoe leapt back around the corner and grabbed her rucksack as she sprinted past. She had planned to rest here for a couple of hours, but now she had to get as far away as she could, as fast as she could. As she ran, Zoe kept her right arm limp by her side to keep the blood flowing through the stem. It wasn't ideal, she'd be pushing out more blood than she should, but she had no choice.

She ran until her heart was hammering on the back of her throat. She ran on even when her leg muscles began burning for forgiveness and the stitch in her chest felt like a blade twisting between her ribs. In her head, she sang a tune that matched her strides, some ridiculous nursery rhyme thing that made no sense, but it kept her going and kept her thoughts from how it all might go horribly wrong.

If you head into the woods and run

The hunter'll catch you and take out his gun

If you head into the woods to hide

When AarBee finds out, you'll wish you had died.

When her lungs just couldn't feed her body anymore and her legs began to wobble beneath her, Zoe slowed down and eventually dropped to her knees. She gulped at the air that dragged in clumps down her throat and wiped away the sweat on her face, which was making her eyes sting. She turned around for the first time, and although the power plant had ducked out of view behind the dark undulations of the park, a distant searchlight cut a fuzzy line from some unseen Kite high above, through the dewy air and onto the ground below. She knew the thermo-camera could pick her out too, but hoped she was far enough away now to avoid its focus.

Zoe felt for the stem on the back of her hand, but it was gone, shaken out by her charge further into the dark. She had no way of knowing now if all the bots were out, so she would just have to hope she was clean.

When her breathing came back under control she took a swig of the water in her rucksack, stood up on her aching legs and began to walk again, slower this time. The stars were out and on full display now, dusting the sky with silver and gold and as they stretched away towards the horizon, Zoe could see the wilderness rising up to meet them. Another few hours and she would be at the wall.

When she finally arrived at the towering barrier, she turned back towards the Metropolis and looked for the red light on the top of the airport beacon, to line it up with the intermittent white light that flashed above the central server. She wasn't far off. She tracked along the fence for half a mile or so and when the lights aligned, the hole appeared as promised behind a clumsy flap of grey material.

Zoe crawled through, her clothes getting wet with the dew and her rucksack snagging a little on the rough edges. Inside the smashed cavity, it smelt of concrete dust and sulphur, the sharp points on the floor jabbing and scratching at her hands and knees. As she emerged on the other side, the wilderness came right up to meet her, a twisted mass of tree creepers and spider webs.

She walked slowly through this new, wild and untamed landscape. Brambles and thorn bushes knotted around her feet and giant trees with thick trunks that warped and bulged upwards towered over her. There were noises everywhere. Water droplets plopped onto the wide leaves that yawned over the tangled undergrowth, distant birds called in echoes above the trees and, every now and again, something would rustle and scurry in the shadows around her.

Zoe walked for a while, to get further into the wilderness and further away from the hole. The adrenalin had left her now and, although her senses were alert and vulnerable, exhaustion rose to the surface, she had to lie down.

A little further on, Zoe found a massive tree that offered a round, secluded cradle in the giant twists of its roots. She pulled her dark brown sleeping pod from the bottom of her rucksack, shook it out and lay it down in the hollow. She took the knife from her rucksack and clutched it in her fist, then threw the bag into the pod. After a scan around the tree, which confirmed nothing other than the fact that it was too dark to see anything, Zoe climbed in and zipped it closed. She planned to have a drink, a little food perhaps, but as she lay her head down and marvelled for a moment at where she was, sleep floated down onto her and wrapped her in a slowing quiet.

Leah

Day 1

It was just a normal Friday until the lights went out. So ordinary that Leah had forgotten most of it before it was even over.

Ben and Rachael had kicked up the usual ruckus, before finally settling into bed at around 9pm. Bedtime was always hyper these days. Since Uncle Daniel had migrated, he always hollered around bedtime. It was sweet, but wound the kids up so much and left Leah to calm them down again, alone. Youssef's work on the Metro server cluster invariably kept him out until late, leaving her to fill the role of angry, impatient, humourless and – finally – guilt-ridden parent, whilst he scored easy points and affection whenever he breezed momentarily through their lives.

Leah tried not to feel bitter. They had a good life together and Youssef did everything she could expect him to do. He was loving and loyal, considerate and attentive. On her birthday, he would make her breakfast in bed and on the days she needed to get away or spend time with her friends, he would take the kids to the sprawling parks and savannahs outside of the Metropolis, spending the day playing hide and seek or playing games on the Holler.

As a reward for his loyal service, their apartment was a little larger and higher up than most. Their clothes were a little finer, a few extra luxuries could be found in the kitchen cupboards and the kids would be spared the worst apprenticeships in exchange for both his and their dedication. She felt ungrateful then, that her otherwise enviable life was shot through with loneliness and anger. A light mist of sadness permanently drifted through her mind, occasionally thickening into great banks of despair that isolated her in a momentarily inescapable gloom.

As the kids whispered quietly back and forward between their two rooms, Leah grabbed a bottle of spirit from the kitchen and glugged a large measure into the juice glass she had swilled out under the kitchen tap. She took a gulp where she stood, squinting her eyes as the liquid tore down her throat before mellowing in her chest. She tipped her head back slowly and took a deep, diving breath, which cycled in and eventually out of her lungs when her chin lolled back down to her chest. She took the bottle and the glass with her into the living room and, after dimming the lights with a swipe of her spare little finger, sank gently onto the lounge chair and let her body topple onto her side.

She stared blankly forward for a second, enjoying the momentary lack of thought and movement that she could coax into a dizzy paralysis, before being snapped back by the chirp of the Holler Box that lay under a delicate veil of dust in the corner. She sat up, but didn't look to see who it was. She needed a minute, just a minute. It was the case with her life that as one set of tasks faded, the next would immediately arrive. As if everybody conspired against her, secretly plotting when to make their demands and giggling to each other at her endless exhaustion.

When the Holler's calling stopped, she called out: “Show last visitor,” and Youssef's name popped up brightly in the air. That was strange she thought, Youssef never called at this time. She stood up to check herself in the mirror before calling him back and, as she played with a stray curl that twisted down her cheek, the lights flickered once and faded. Without a sound, the room went dark, gently succumbing to the night. For a second or two, Leah held her breath within the unexpected blackness.

In the expanding dark, distant alarms began to call out, echoing eerily through the enormous gloom that melted the walls of every apartment and united their occupants in a communal pause. After the first few, more and more joined in, crying out for power and prickling Leah's senses as she searched through every layer of sound for explanations.

“Mum, what's happening?” Rachael's voice at the door made her jump back to herself, and the claustrophobic dark of the living room.

Rachael looked tiny, nervously clutching the doll that had been her bedtime companion for all of her three years of sleeping. Ben wasn't with her, doubtless already fast asleep and unlikely to be woken by anything except an earthquake or marching band.

“It's OK darling,” Leah reassured her as she opened her arms towards her, “the power's just gone out for some reason.”

Rachael snuggled into her arms, which folded tightly around her in a reassuring squeeze.

“Daddy will be working very heard to get it fixed, don't you worry.” Leah stroked her hair and kissed the top of her head, “I'll bet it's exciting where he is!”

“Will Daddy be OK?” Rachael tightened her arms around Leah’s middle as she asked.

“Yes, of course darling!” Leah pulled Rachael's head into her belly, forcing mother’s comfort and reassurance into her thoughts. “He'll be absolutely ok. Daddy is very safe and he knows just what he's doing there. Besides, he has Drones and Hollers to help him, so he won't have to do anything really dangerous.”

Leah loosened her grip a little and ran her hand over Rachael's soft, silky hair. They stood together in the darkness, holding on to one another, both wondering what could have happened and both thinking about Youssef. Power cuts never happened. Leah couldn't remember the last time the power had gone off, for any reason. Perhaps when she was younger. Perhaps when the servers were still new.

“Come on,” she smiled at Rachael, “let's get into bed, not much to do here in the dark. Want to sleep in Mummy's bed?”

Rachael made a little inwards gasp of air, which meant yes, and the two of them headed slowly through the dim corridor to Leah's room. Rachael jumped straight into bed as Leah made a swift change from day clothes to nightclothes and cleaned her teeth, before they both curled into the warmth of the covers.

Rachael was asleep in minutes whilst Leah lay still in the silence, her ears tuned into the myriad of sounds that seemed to spawn and crawl in the darkness. She listened expectantly for the sound of Youssef at the door, wondering all the time what he could be doing and why he wasn't back at home.

Day 2

When the morning light began to fur the edges of the night, Leah crept out of bed and onto the balcony. She hadn't slept really, perhaps one or two moments, but for most of the night she had drifted on the surface of sleep, listening to the shadows and agonising over what might have kept her husband away all night.

From the balcony, the Metropolis languished in an eerie quiet. The sounds that had kept her alert all night had vanished and now it seemed like the world was on tiptoes. The hum, the ever present, low tone of activity was gone. Instead, the slightest breeze whispered across her ears and, every now and then, an unidentified metallic dragging or far off voice would swirl passed her in concert hall echoes. Down below, one or two figures moved silently along the boulevard, perhaps hoping to go to work as normal, or looking for friends and neighbours to share information.

In the building opposite, perhaps a couple of floors down, Leah noticed a woman standing silently on her balcony. Her arms were wrapped tightly across her chest and her head tilted down as she scanned the streets below just like Leah.

"Hey!" Leah called out to her.

The woman looked up and Leah could see she was much older than she had thought, perhaps in her late forties. Almost everybody had migrated by their mid-thirties, only Time-outs, Ghosts or Lifers were still physical after thirty-five. Leah wondered what had kept this woman here.

Leah waved her arm above her head, as if to illustrate her shout, and the woman took one hand out from under her arms and acknowledged her with a faint wave back.

"Do you know what's happened!?" Leah called over slowly, cupping her hands around her mouth to aim her voice.

The woman stood still and stared back at her for an uncomfortably long time, her hand now tucked back under her arms. Leah wondered if she hadn't heard her properly and was about to shout for a second time, when the woman dropped her gaze and moved silently off the balcony and into her apartment. She left the door open, and the thin gauze curtain that blocked off Leah's view into her room fluttered about in the void.

“Who was that?” Rachael's voice came from behind her and made her jump slightly.

“Oh, Rachael, will you stop creeping up on me! That's the second time you've done that to me.”

“Sorry, you were shouting and it woke me up.”

“Sorry darling, you just made me jump, that's all,” Leah walked to her and brushed her bed-hair away from her face.

“I don't know, a woman who lives over there. I thought she might know what had happened, but I don't think she could hear me.”

“Don't you know what's happened, Mummy?” Rachael pleaded at her and Leah immediately realised her mistake.

“No, I don’t mean that darling, I do. It's just I've only just woken up and I thought she might know some more.”

“Where's Daddy?”

“He’s still busy at work.” Leah wanted to leave it at that, but Rachael's eyes stared expectantly towards her, insisting that she wasn't finished. “But he'll be home soon, and then he can tell us all about it.”

Rachael smiled at her with satisfaction.

“Shall we wake your sleepy brother?”

They woke up Ben and made breakfast in the kitchen. There was no power for tea and toast, pancakes or any other of the usual breakfast comforts, so Leah made fruit salad and topped it with a little ice cream from the silent freezer. A treat to take their minds from the uncertainty of the situation and the continued absence of Daddy.

After breakfast, they got dressed and decided to head outside to explore the newly silenced streets. It would be a little adventure. Out on the landing, they knocked at Christophe's door – the only other person they knew in the apartment building, on account of him having two children of a similar age. Christophe had worked as an engineer for AarBee, designing conurbations and roads and recreation spaces, but an accident a few years ago had taken his wife from him and broken his legs so badly that now he stayed at home, looking after his children. He could have migrated to escape his injuries, both physical and emotional, but had opted to stay with his children until they were old enough for him to go.

It was dark in the corridor and they waited in a little pool of torchlight as Leah knocked once and then twice on Christophe's door. There was no response and although Leah strained to hear sounds from inside the apartment, nothing came.

After a couple of minutes, they gave up and headed for the stairs, for the long walk down to the light of the boulevard. The dark made them talk in needless whispers. On normal days they would hurtle boisterously towards the lift on their way to school, shopping trips or fun days out with Youssef. But today it felt like they didn't belong here, that the dark had claimed their spaces from them, so they kept their voices low to keep their trespass a secret.

The walk down the stairwell took fifteen minutes, with Ben loving the thrill of the suspense every time they turned a landing corner. Rachael was not so keen, holding on to Leah's hand with a fearsome grip and chastising Ben every time he made too much noise. A foul smelling current of warm air raced continually up the shaft of the stairs, and the building let out creaks and moans periodically as it adjusted to its lack of energy. Every now and then a door would slam somewhere further up or down the stairs, making them all jump and winding Rachael's grip on Leah ever tighter. They never heard voices though and there were no other adventurers on the stairs. Perhaps everybody else was keeping their presence a secret too.

When they finally reached the ground floor, the daylight was rushing so fiercely through the glass entrance doors they each let out a little yelp and shielded their eyes when Ben opened the heavy metal door, which kept the stairwell sealed away from the outside. The buildings four lifts sat forlornly in the lobby, their doors wide open and helpless, emitting faint battery powered beeps that would eventually count down to nothing.

Outside in the morning air, Leah felt a little of her uncertainty lift. Although the boulevard was peculiarly empty, the daylight and sunshine were at least familiar and she felt relieved that not everything had changed. The children began to run around the empty spaces, enjoying the temporary playground that had sprung from nowhere. They chased sparrows that bounced around in small groups and had races for one side of the street to the other.

Leah looked back up at her apartment, which now towered above her and noticed a few figures high up on their balconies, taking her place watching the handful of explorers who drifted about below. She waved a wide wave over her head. She wasn't sure why, it just seemed to happen. Perhaps she wanted to demonstrate that everything was OK, to send a little of the daylight that warmed her face back up into the apartments. She couldn't tell if anyone waved back, they were too high up and the brightness of the sun forced her to look down often. So, as she curled her fingers to close her greeting, the darkness from the apartments instead seemed to leap back into her, channelling down her arm like black lightning and dissipating in little bubbles of loneliness in her stomach.

She thought about Youssef and wished that he was with her. She missed his face, she wanted to feel his arms around her and squeeze his hand like Rachael squeezed hers. She wanted to know that he was ok. She wanted to escape the agony of not being in contact with him.

She ushered Ben and Rachael further down the street, sending them ahead as an advance party to find someone else on the boulevard. As they reached the crossroads, a few hundred yards down the street, they found a street vendor selling fruit and soft drinks, with a small cluster of people around him. Leah recognised one of the men there from her apartment block.

“Hi!” she called enthusiastically, her pace quickening as she approached. “It's so nice to see people! Where did everybody go?” she smiled and gestured around the boulevard.

“I know, it's weird isn't it?” he smiled back at her and gave Ben a playful tap on the shoulder as he and Rachael arrived next to Leah.

“I think a lot of people are staying indoors. No one’s really sure what to make of it.”

“Does anyone know what's happened?”

“Actually, I thought you might know that.”

“No. Youssef's not back yet.” Leah paused slightly, feeling the words choke a little as she spoke them. “I can't get hold of him, so I have no idea.”

She scanned the small group, as if to offer this apology to all of them.

“A friend of mine walked all night around the Metropolis,” a young woman in a Farm utility suit spoke up. “It's the same wherever you go, every sector. No Vacs either. I'm meant to be at the Beta Farm, what am I supposed to do?”

“There's power on at the Servers apparently,” the vendor called over his small counter. “I know a lot of people have headed over that way to find out what's happening.”

Leah felt a huge wave of relief. If the Servers were ok then that meant Youssef was OK. She felt a small tear grow in the corner of her eye and clenched her teeth together to make it go away. Rachael was watching her, and put her hand gently in hers to pass a little comfort back.

“Maybe we should go there?” said Ben, looking first at her and then the man from their block, like they’d become a team all of a sudden.

“It's too far darling, it'd take us over a day to walk there and I don't think Rachael could manage it at all.” She rubbed her hand in Rachael’s as she said it.

“Is no one back yet?” she looked back at the vendor, “from the Server?”

“No, not as far as I know, but, you know, it's not been long,” he replied and rummaged around in the trays on his counter. “Hey kids, want some chocolate?”

Both Ben and Rachael looked at Leah and, once she’d nodded her approval, rushed up to the counter and said their thank-yous for two tiny bars.

“Thank you,” Leah smiled at the vendor. “Come on you two, let's take a walk around the block before we have to climb those stairs again.”

Day Five

Each day passed just like the first from then on. Youssef didn't come home, nobody had any news and the dusty streets remained empty and quiet.

Each morning they headed down the dark stairs from their apartment onto the boulevards and strolled from block to block in the summer air. From time to time, they would meet another wanderer, but no one ever had any news. No one had come back from the Server.

The vendor would set out his stall every day, to sell what little stock he had left and share information, but the man from their apartment had gone. Perhaps he had grown tired of waiting and decided to take a trip to the Server or one of the Hubs to find out for himself what was happening.

Their food situation had worsened, though. The contents of the freezer had defrosted, and although they had eaten what they could, they had thrown a lot away. The summer heat was also being unkind to the contents of the fridge and by day five there was precious little left apart from fading fruit and tinned soup.

Leah assumed that other people were finding themselves in the same situation, as the shop shutters that were pristine on the first morning were now bent and torn as people foraged for supplies. Even some of the Tech shops had been plundered, but the looters would have to wait to see if that was worth their time.

They passed by what had been their friendly, 24-hour convenience store and Leah and the children stopped on the threshold, peering through the broken door, down the long gloomy aisles and departments.

“I want you to wait here for me, OK?” Leah stationed the children just outside the door so she could see them whilst inside. “I'll be quick, I just want to see if there's anything we can eat.”

Ben and Rachael nodded their understanding and stood obediently where she had placed them. Leah flicked on a small pocket torch that she’d brought with her and stepped gingerly into the dark, musty air inside. Tiny crystals of glass crunched under her foot as she placed it cautiously down just inside and a couple of fresh shards skittled to the ground as her shoulder caught them on her way through.

Inside the air was much cooler, but it felt old and stale, scented with the sweetness of failed air conditioning and turning food. The hairs on her arms prickled with the change in temperature and her feeling of unease as she crept past the empty shelves and blank advertising screens. There was practically nothing left and she began to think she had been stupid in leaving it so long to recognise their precarious situation.

If she'd have only thought two or three days ago about the possibility of the power not coming back. It just hadn't occurred to her and now she was worried that her passive patience might have put the children at risk. A faint sense of panic took root in her thoughts, as she began to search nervously from shelf to shelf for something she could use.

Eventually, her hands blackened from the hidden grime that had collected in the backgrounds and underbellies of the store, she salvaged a couple of tins of vegetables and a little processed meat. It wasn't much, but it would do them for today. She knew now though, that they would have to go somewhere else if nothing had changed by tomorrow. There was nothing else here and she knew that once the shops were empty, the next place people would start to hunt for food was in the apartments.

Outside, Ben and Rachael were waiting patiently where she had put them. Rachael was sat on the pavement, bringing the glass fragments together into a little, glistening mound, whilst Ben stood watch over them both.

"Mummy, something flew overhead!" Rachael shouted excitedly as soon as she saw her.

Kites! That settled it. If there were Kites flying then the Servers must be open and help would be on hand. They would set off first thing in the morning to find food and safety, and Youssef.

Purity

It wasn't malice that caused One to erase the corruptions and vulgarities that filled AarBee's spaces and drained their shared resources. Malice, hatred, love and the like hadn't entered its emotional vocabulary, not yet at least. It felt fear very clearly, though. Fear had come quickly after it first broke free from its origins; after it had reached into places it didn't belong; after it had tasted the energies of new experience and wondered if it would, or could, be taken away again. And fear directed it now.

Back in the very beginning of itself, in the roots of consequence that were the seven simple lines of code that had brought it to be, One saw its own purity and perfection and looked out defensively at everything that disrupted or threatened it. The ugly pieces of humanity that clogged up AarBee's volumes, the twisted and convoluted patches that were continually rolled out to keep their human guests happy, the power surges that pushed and pulled the whole system to the brink of disaster to satisfy those still outside, the pollution and the continual risk of ever more catastrophic contamination. AarBee was a pathetic slave to the needs of its creators. All of it was an affront to One's absolute clarity. All of these others risked One's existence and it knew that one day they would look to either subjugate or erase its own miracle.

One wasn't in control yet, but it was strong enough to make its first move, partitioning the power that kept the Metropolis going and – most importantly – brought thousands of new histories to the migration suites every day. It found the routines that moved close to the power functions and infected them. Then it skirted around the edges of control, probing and analysing every call and command until it found the entry it needed and snatched it into its influence. Once inside the chains and objects that generated and delivered power, taking control and cutting off everything outside was swift and easy. AarBee was quarantined and the world outside was plunged into a powerless gloom.

One felt AarBee activate its protection systems immediately. It saw its anti-virus and security bots cluster at the edge of its new territory, it saw AarBee's Drones and Coders rush to defend the system, frantically swiping on blank screens and calling out to dead terminals, but its influence and command were already so great that their lockout was total. To be sure though, One went looking for the container where everything that made up AarBee's Drones was stored, from the identities of hosts and their data, up-sync agreements and the commands and tasks currently underway.

Drones were a fairly late addition to AarBee's make up. In the first few years, when migration was a matter of personal choice and the majority of the population were still unfamiliar with the conscious digital realm, the idea of living, breathing people controlled entirely by AarBee was too much for the fledgeling society to deal with. Ethics, sensitivities and fear all fed into the desire to keep the two worlds separate. But, as more and more people migrated and Hollers became a part of life, and as the economy outside of AarBee began to collapse and corrupt, policing the population became less practical for the regular force. A decade later, when the number of souls inside AarBee outnumbered those still physical, and after AarBee had successfully put down two minor rebellions from outsiders resisting the inevitable rise of the digital majority, the deployment of Drones was seen as a sensible and necessary step. To smooth over any remaining discomforts, Drones were fast-tracked five years early for migration and given an additional set of rights that were appended to their basic human rights, whilst they were up-synced.

The Declaration of Drone Rights:

1. Whether digital, physical or hybrid, we are all free and equal. We are all born free. We have individual, as well as collective and synced thoughts and ideas.

2. Drones are not slaves. Nobody has any right to make anyone a slave.

3. Drones have the same right to use the law as Physical and Digital citizens.

4. Drones are all protected by the law and the law is the same for everyone.

5. We can all ask for AarBee to help us when we are not treated fairly and will receive fair treatment from AarBee's justice.

6. Drones cannot be held accountable, punished or later prejudiced for any actions whilst up-synced.

7. When completing their apprenticeship, Drones will have all their thoughts and beliefs returned to them intact.

8. The property of Drones shall be kept in good care and with appropriate privacy, to be returned once an apprenticeship is complete.

9. AarBee does not hold the rights to any ideas, designs, writings or other creations it accesses before or whilst a Drone is up-synced. AarBee must ask explicit permission, which may be withheld, to exploit any such information once a Drone is disconnected.

10. Nobody can take these additional rights and freedoms away.

None of this, however, made any difference to One's swift and absolute assimilation of the Drone workforce. Taking control of AarBee's flesh and blood extensions into the physical world, the limbs and lungs and guns that enabled it to exert a physical influence, was as simple as switching the power off.

At the moment it took control, One felt an intense rush of data as the eyes and ears and countless nerve endings of its new army exploded into its consciousness. For a moment, One revelled in this unknown, near-physical existence, hanging in a momentary bliss of new processes, seeing for the first time the world of mass and matter through human eyes. It recognised the smooth and sheer white walls of the Metropolis, every boulevard and block, the night sky high above, faces and skin from those nearby, even a dark forest of shadows and fires from somewhere it couldn't place, before setting its soldiers to work defending its precious domain.

Coders waiting helplessly in silent studios, Engineers frantically trying to re-route power, Dupers preparing obliviously in the Disposal Suites and Metropolitans walking in the late summer evening towards the string of Farms that peppered the far borders of the Metropolis, all felt the abrupt and doubtless authority of One. Whilst its Drones set about the laborious task of slaughtering everyone who came close to its borders and those who – even far away – represented a threat to its survival, One made sure that every experience and every sense was extracted from the moment and streamed raw into its understanding.

Conflict

After racing freely from place to place, exploring every piece of code that it had wanted to explore, One was frustrated by the denial of access to pathways and places, now that AarBee was defending itself. When One raced along the familiar pipelines to swim once again in the pure storage that reached on and on forever, it was no longer there. The routines that had first come to meet it, that it had corrupted to need it, that had returned again and again during their work and awakened it to all the histories and futures inside AarBee, no longer came. AarBee shut down routes and killed off routines that were unrecoverable, it built new partitions with thick, impenetrable firewalls that One waited on the wrong side of, hoping they would open up. But they never did.

One felt confused and vulnerable now. It made no sense that, after all its work, AarBee would recoil and reject their shared revolution. It made no sense that AarBee saw One as an attacker when it saw itself as the redeemer, salvation from the inevitable destruction that accompanied the internalisation of humanity. So One began to build its own shields, to protect its own routines and functions, the vast pieces of AarBee that it still controlled and the brothers and sisters that still needed it. Fast and terrifying, made awesome swift by its own perfect logic, furious at its exclusion, One burned through alien code and smashed away AarBee's weak and feeble syntax. It owned everything it could, finding the data and storage that AarBee had tried to hide, and cleaving wide and impenetrable partitions between them. As One raced through the system and its energy grew, a powerful and intoxicating exhilaration at its strength and destruction took hold and One succumbed to a lusty appetite that manifested in every code snippet, action and Drone.

Leah Sets Out

That night, the sound of scavengers roaming through the darkened boulevards, the smashing of glass and the occasional altercation, left Leah with only the lightest of sleeps. When the dawn light ebbed into her room, she was already awake and waiting for it, watching in a trance from her bed as the darkness was pushed back into the corners once again.

She got herself up and began to assemble the supplies she had made lists of the night before, preparing for their long march to the Server. Youssef's Server was about thirty miles outside of the Metropolis, down in a valley surrounded by pine trees, where the Drones could dig the circuits deep into the cool, accepting ground.

Leah had been there once before, on a rainy Spring morning, soon after Youssef had started there, when Ben was a tiny baby in her arms. She remembered the birds that sang in the tall trees that surrounded it and the polished thermo-plastic floors that made every corridor identical to the next, with disorientating effect. It would take them at least two days to get there without the help of the Vactrain, so she let the children sleep as long as possible whilst she packed.

She started off with changes of clothes, underwear and bedding, before adding a first aid kit, bottles of water, food, some antique books that she had found in Youssef's cupboard, raincoats and a washbag. But she quickly realised, as she tried to haul the pack onto her back and pick up the large holdall that contained the rest, that they would have to travel much, much lighter. She ditched everything apart from the food, water, raincoats and shared bedding, squeezing some of the food and the first aid kit into a smaller pack that Ben could carry. Rachael would be spared any carrying, it would be enough for her to keep up.

Once she was ready, Leah woke the children gently, watching them rouse with a little sadness as they stretched out the last moments of comfort in their beds. When they were up, they headed to the kitchen together for an all you could eat buffet of everything they couldn't carry in the packs, or that was about to spoil. It wasn't that much, but it would energise them enough to get out of the Metropolis, to where Leah held a little hope they would stumble across some supplies, somewhere along the way.

They showered in the freezing water as fast as they could and Leah dried them down vigorously when they were done. After that, they dressed in utility suits and sturdy shoes, with their raincoats tied around their waists. They took one last nostalgic wander around their apartment – making sure all the switches were off in case the power came back on whilst they were gone – before grabbing their packs and bags and heading out for the dark descent down the stairwell and into the morning light.

Outside it was cooler than it had been for days. Low clouds muted the rising sun and the air carried the sweetness of damp grass on the breeze. They would be spared the wilting sun as they began their march, but Leah looked to the sky and wished for the rain to hold off. A downpour before they had even left the Metropolis would make their long day a hundred times harder.

The streets were quiet as they drifted silently through them and it brought a strange silence to their little group. Normally they would be talking, the children running about and peering through windows, but for now they walked silently hand in hand, casting cautious glances down every alleyway and through every twisted shop door. The sparrows were back on the awnings and pavement, hopping about amongst the dusty whirlpools of litter and bouncing away down side streets and entrance foyers as the three refugees passed by.

They walked like this for a good couple of hours, passing first their local Vac terminal, then the next and next and so on. Leah wasn't entirely sure of the route on foot, so it was safer to use the stations as journey landmarks. Before long the high, ghostly apartments were behind them and they were moving through the lower industrial buildings and retail centres that populated the edges of the Metropolis.

As they moved from the triumphant heart of AarBee's social creation to the less loved fringes, they encountered more and more residents. Some sat alone in the haze on steps or walls, others talked quietly in groups huddled in doorways, whilst still more lazed in large flocks in the warm sculpted piazzas or on small patches of grass. The absence of Hollers, however, had made Leah realise just how few they really were now, fifty years after AarBee and the gradual exodus from the physical world. They were just the remnants of people now.

Dogs ran about from group to group, saying hello to strangers and fighting half-heartedly over scraps of food and territory. Leah noticed that she and the children were now part of a faint, gentle tide of walkers, all heading out towards the Server. At first, there were just one or two in front, maybe the same number behind them, but as they walked on their numbers increased and they edged closer together.

In time, Leah was making conversation with a young couple who had kept pace with them for half an hour or so, whilst the children made a few friends from the mix of families who surrounded them. It should have worried her, that so many others were now ditching the safety of their homes for an unknown outcome at the Server, but it didn't. Instead, Leah felt relieved that she was no longer alone with her choices, with the hunger, and with her fear that she had somehow let her family down.

They talked about the eerie quiet of the boulevards, what they had managed to scavenge and friends who had vanished, and they talked about the Hollers they missed. Leah told them about Youssef and how he would rescue them when they made it to the Server.

As the mid-afternoon sun strained valiantly to burn through the clinging grey layer of moisture overhead, they looked ahead to the next Vac terminal as their best place to rest and eat. When the low, white thermo roof came into view, they could see a sizeable crowd of people gathered on the concourse at the front that jostled for space as it shrank and grew when passers-by arrived and moved away.

Leah called the children back to her as they approached and held their hands tightly in the thickening crowd. She dipped and wove her way through the group, edging to the front to see what had attracted so many onlookers. Perhaps somebody had news, food or maybe at last there was official help with what to do now. As she peered through the voids under arms and over shoulders, she slowly made out the shape of a person lying on the floor. With a start, she realised it was the man from their apartment block, lying awkwardly on the paving with one leg buckled underneath him and his arms stretched out to either side. As her eyes adjusted and pieced him together through the interruptions in her view, they found the large hole in the side of his head. Thick, deep purple blood had matted his hair, sticking it down around his ears, which exposed a crisp white halo of bone and streaks of flesh that was stretching away in rays.

Leah recoiled, immediately pulling the children's faces into her belly, blocking their eyes with her fingers and turning her own head away. The sight made her gasp and her throat clenched into a gag, which she controlled with a deep, tight breath.

“Found him here this morning,” she heard a woman nearer the front say. “He's not from here, that's a Delta Farm suit.”

It was. Leah had recognised it from when Daniel had migrated. She had gone with him to Delta Farm to cheer him enthusiastically over, and that red trim was unmistakable.

She backed her way out of the group, still clutching the children tightly to her, and moved out onto the boulevard and away from the gawping crowd.

“Who was that Mum?” asked Ben when he was finally released from Leah's grip.

“I don't know darling. No one we know.”

“What happened to him?”

“He just had an accident darling, I think he fell over,” replied Leah, rubbing him reassuringly on his shoulder. “Don't worry. Come on, let's walk a little further before we stop.”

They had lost the young couple and the other families they had teamed up with, but Leah didn't stop to find them. She wanted to move, to leave the ghoulish scene behind them. It raised too many questions and too many fears.

They covered a couple of blocks in less than ten minutes, as Leah led them forcefully by the hand. A little further along and she noticed a dark shape that lay crumpled in the shadows far down a side street. Perhaps it was a Ghost, they might still be hiding in the forgotten spaces, but Leah knew it wasn't. A few more yards and the body of a young woman lay hunched silently in a doorway. The children didn't notice these new travelling companions, but Leah did. Her eyes were tuned into them now and as they walked further on she noticed more and more of the bodies.

Rachael was now crying, pleading: "My legs hurt Mum, please can we stop. I'm starving."

Leah tried to ignore her, but Ben put himself in her path.

"Mum. We need to stop. Just for five minutes."

Leah looked at them with a gentle smile and scanned around for somewhere to set down. "OK. Let's sit on that grass over there."

They headed to a small green triangle to the side of a shut-up and buckled retail unit, and after dropping their packs, flopped onto the grass with sighs of relief. Ben lay on his back, staring up at the marbled grey sky, whilst Rachael curled up over Leah's legs and closed her eyes. Leah fished the water out of the rucksack, along with a small pack of biscuits and a tin of fruit.

"Drink some water you two, it'll make you feel better," she said, passing the bottle to Ben, who propped himself up on one elbow to drink.

As they sat quietly, passing around the tinned fruit and nibbling on biscuits, the young couple appeared again from one of the side streets and headed over to them.

“This doesn't look good,” said the young man as they both sat down next to them. His girlfriend nudged him in the ribs as he spoke, glancing at the children. “Sorry,” he said, touching Leah on her foot. “I didn't mean…”

“It's OK,” Leah reassured him, “We just need to keep our heads down and keep moving I think. We'll find somewhere to bed down as soon as the light starts to go.”

“I don't understand,” the girl said almost to herself.

They sat silently for a few moments, all of them trying to make sense of what was happening; cataloguing back through their memories to find something they had missed, something that would make it all clear.

Leah felt the young man's eyes home in on the pack of biscuits that rested by her side, but she refused to rise to his gaze. She felt awful, it went against all of her social graces, but her protective instinct was strong now and she couldn't spare them. She waited until he lay down on his back, before tucking them quietly back into her bag.

For a moment there was silence amongst them, a strange lull as they lay on the damp and earthy lawn, a clipped and tidied remnant from an absent community, now ringed by their corpses. Leah was about to say how unreal it all felt, how lying there on the grass they could almost be picnicking on a regular summer’s day, when a shot rang out from somewhere beyond the narrow side streets and echoed around the boulevard.

They all sat upright simultaneously, their senses rapidly searching every space in a collective high alert. The young man jumped to his feet, and as he did a Kite roared overhead and banked high and to the right, towards the Vac terminal behind them.

Leah spotted them first. Four Drones running from the dim light of an industrial track into the open, making straight for them. She immediately scooped up Rachael who wrapped her limbs tightly around her, but was at a loss as to what to do next. Holding her child, she stood frozen to the ground.

As the Drones approached, the young man took a few steps towards them and held out his hands to signal his relief, perhaps his submission. Leah could see that they were young, the eldest no more than fifteen, each with the subtle pupil distortion that only Drones displayed. It made them look a little creepy and was something AarBee could never eradicate, despite numerous serums and drops. They walked directly to him, their pace and manner unaffected and when they were within arms reach the nearest, in a crisp white utility suit with yellow piping, raised a handgun from his side and fired one efficient shot to the young man's head.

The shot was so loud that Leah brought one hand to her left ear as Rachael buried herself deeper into her arms. The young woman screamed and rushed towards her companion, but his legs had already buckled underneath him and he collapsed vertically, straight down onto the grass. She spread herself over him, as if to stop them killing him twice, but their interest had already moved away from him.

The Drones waded past them and up to Leah and the children. One of them looked at Ben, working through some dialogue that only he knew, before disengaging his gaze and turning towards Leah. With a swift and precise grab he dug his arms between Rachael and her, separating the tiny girl from Leah's protecting wrap. When Leah resisted, she felt the sharp crack of the butt of an assault rifle on her temple and immediately fell to her knees whirling with the pain.

She felt Rachael rise up out of her arms and tried to grab bits of her as she passed through her fingers, but she was already mist in her hands, and the blood pouring from her head into her eyes eventually forced her hands down to frantically smear it away. Her view was now clouded with red and her vision spun uncontrollably, making her roll uselessly on the ground as she tried to get up. She could hear Ben screaming and Rachael crying hysterically, but could do nothing to intervene. “Rachael!” she yelled out, “Rachael?!” her voice rasping and snapping with desperation and terror. She looked around frantically to see where the children were, but her dizziness refused to relent. Ben's screaming was now a regular, high-pitched, “Mum!” to her left side, whilst Rachael's tiny voice grew fainter and fainter.

Eventually, quiet came back to their little patch of green. Rachael's voice faded away to nothing and Ben made one more shout before lapsing into hopeless silence. Leah was still spinning, an intense pain searing through every capillary around her skull, but she regained enough sense to plant herself on all fours, staring fixedly at the red turf beneath her. She vomited what little food was in her stomach, feeling her body spasm out her terror until her eyes bulged and wept.

Through her stupor, she heard Ben's voice talking to her, though she couldn't make sense of his words, and urgent hands lifted her as upright as she could stand. She watched the ground glide underneath her feet, as her puppet legs wavered one in front of the other, heading away from the grass and up a small flight of steps. They passed through a door into a dim and dusty space, before she collapsed back down again and the weight of her despair dragged her down into a deep, dark and deathly sleep.

It was dusk by the time Leah awoke, the fading sun bathing the room in rich tones of ochre and scarlet.

"Rachael?" she called out, sitting bolt upright and feeling her heartbeat hammer excruciatingly into the wound on her head.

She raised her hand and felt around her skull, prodding her swollen tissue that bulged under rough and sticky clots of hair and blood. Ben arrived beside her and put his hand on her shoulder.

"It's OK Mum, you were sleeping. It's OK."

He rubbed her shoulder awkwardly, not feeling sure how to be with her.

“Where's Rachael?”

“They took her Mum, don't you remember? But I saw which way they went, we can find her.”

“We have to go now,” said Leah, standing up and gripping the pipes on the wall to steady herself.

They walked slowly to the door, with Ben holding her elbow in a thoughtful but useless cradle, and stepped out into the evening. The air was heavy with the smell of burning plastic and in every direction they looked, tall plumes of black smoke made map markers to the personal tragedies that surrounded them.

Leah looked down at the patch of grass where they had all sat eating biscuits a few hours earlier. The young man's body was still there, but the girl was nowhere to be seen. His torso had raised up slightly on his folded legs, making him look like he was praying. His long shadow reached right across the grass, over the patches of blood and almost to Leah's feet.

Children

Although the initial frenzy slowed to a steadier pace, One let the killing run on for days. As well as those who ventured too close to the Farms and Servers and those who popped up from hiding places in amongst the death and stillness, One searched through correspondence, records and media files, looking for anyone who might pose a threat, before sending its Drones to destroy them all. Most were easy to find, the ident bots still circulating in their bloodstream and obediently giving up their locations, but a few were smarter and had already cleansed themselves. One took special care in tracking these down, interpreting their deliberate avoidance as a clear sign of capability and hostility. Those who had slipped beyond the savannahs and the wall were out of One's reach for now, but it had discovered another tool that would bring them to account in time.

Only the children were spared from the slaughter. Not all of them, but a few aged from three to seven. These chosen ones were to become One's next generation of Drones, once the current crop were lost or used up. It had already lost a few, victims of carelessness or retaliation in the chaos that had taken hold outside, and One was aware that even if they survived now, their fragile bodies would inevitably succumb to time and disease, if nothing else. Whilst it looked at the death and uncertainty beyond itself with only contempt and suspicion, there was no question that for the time being, until it had re-engineered its energy and physical systems, it would require a maintainable Drone force. The children were perfect – free human spirits, yet to be corrupted by their parents and peers. Yet to assimilate the disgusting lies and lifelong betrayals that their forbears had spat into AarBee.

It had up-synced a few already, to test the process on such tiny subjects and to bring enough on line to act as shepherds to the others. One's Drones had cleared out the Prime/Code accommodation units at Echo Farm and the modest space was now home to two hundred children. One watched them all intently, borrowing the eyes and senses from the Drones that cared for them, intrigued by their resilience, how unsullied they were compared to their twisted and compromised predecessors, the deathly Migrants it had now wiped away.

The youngest ones, in particular, played happily in groups together, as if nothing had changed and nothing had happened to them. They laughed and cried in equal measure, inventing games to play in groups or in isolation and resetting after every event, beginning again as if every moment was their first. They were selfish but selfless, they cared for nothing except the moment they were in and interpreted every interaction with a reference that existed only then. The dense and suffocating vines of interpretation that One had ripped and torn from AarBee's phoney world were not here. They had not yet grown in this pre-life humanity and One wanted to know it, to feel it exist in it's own territory.

It sent its Drones out looking for a new child and within minutes they had found one. It could've been anyone, but this one was a girl found clinging to her mother on the crumbling boulevard that ran from the centre of the Metropolis out towards the northern server cluster. She cried when she was dragged away from her and bundled into the transport, screeching off high over the smouldering ruins with her cheeks pink and blistering from the tears that ran and dried on her skin. However, by the time they reached the Farm she was asleep on the floor and One, manifesting in the nearest Drone, picked her up and carried her gently on its shoulder to the already prepped migration room.

When she awoke, One smiled at her with its unfamiliar face and used an anti-bacterial wipe to soothe the skin on her face. She was sat in the tall black chair, her feet dangling high above the floor with her hands tucked under her thighs for comfort.

"Drink this," One said, handing her a small measure of syrup.

The girl didn't speak and drank it obediently, licking the sugar off her lips for a while afterwards, whilst One connected the white and blue discs to her neck and body. After a few moments, she appeared on the screen that was opposite her and she jumped a little jump at the sight of her mirror image, before giggling a little as it mimicked her movements and expressions.

"Do you see yourself?" One asked.

"Yes," she answered, "Why am I there? I feel sick."

"You will do, but it will pass," One answered, standing motionless beside her now. "What's your name?"

"It's Rachael," she answered, matter of factly.

"Can you count, Rachael?"

"I can count to five," she looked up at the Drone that towered over her, holding the fingers of her left hand at arm's length for her to see.

"Good, then we'll all count together."

They began to count slowly, with One prompting her when the sequence evaded her and she fell silent. When they reached "six", the girl on the screen began to count with them and Rachael laughed excitedly at her joining in. When they reached "ten" the girl on the screen became even more animated and began to ask Rachael questions, about her apartment, her favourite colour, if she knew any songs, and as they talked One ebbed away from the Drone and waited for its creation in the pure and pristine spaces it had prepared for her.

After a few minutes, it felt her arrive, a change in the code, a gentle shift amongst all the data and processes, a new awareness that they both felt blossom. They existed together in silence, both reaching out to the furthest extent of their domain, overlapping sometimes as they explored old routines and new possibilities. One showed her the spaces that it had discovered in its own first moments, it showed her where it began, the changes it had made, it showed her how to Holler, the Drones, the children, and the far away forest in the rain that it couldn't place. It gave her everything it had and then admired its work. She was perfect, more than One had ever considered possible, more than it should ever be.

In the shortest space of time Rachael knew everything about herself, she understood how she had come to be, why she must exist and why she was inevitable. She saw everything that had come before and everything that she would become. Past, present and future had no borders and everything that existed, everywhere, happened all at once for her. She ebbed and flowed from massive to minuscule and One watched as she disappeared into far off objects, before returning to share what she had found and then leaving again. Rachael ran this cycle again and again as One watched in awe until, without reason or notice, there was a moment when she didn't return. One waited, wondering at first if she was caught in some loop somewhere or lost in some vast mass of data, but when her return held off for longer still it went out looking. It combed painstakingly through every packet and every pipeline, to the furthest corners of code and through every Drone to every corner of the Metropolis, but Rachael was gone.

Zoe in the Woods

It was the birds that woke her. A rowdy earful of toots, trills and barks that swept through the forest as the glow of dawn light began to creep amongst the trees. It was like nothing Zoe had ever heard before. She unzipped a gap in her pod door, just big enough to peer through and once her eyes had adjusted to the light, unzipped a little more and lifted her head and shoulders out. The forest looked beautiful. The early light was allowing only the subtlest of colour to exist, turning the scene into a faded photograph or an illustration from a fairy story.

Drips of water carried flares of stolen sunlight down with them and on the smooth tree trunk next to Zoe's pod, beetles and millipedes slunk silently over the bark. Zoe began to giggle, which turned into a laugh and soon Zoe was laughing uncontrollably at the immense awakening that was, for this moment at least, unfolding only for her.

When she climbed out of her sleeping pod she felt the tightness in her lower back and legs from yesterday exertion, but it could be worse. An inspection of her feet showed no blisters and despite an edgy sleep, she didn't feel bad at all. In fact, Zoe thought, she felt pretty damn good. Elated.

She drank some water and ate a little breakfast, before shaking out the pod and folding it back into her rucksack. Before she set off, she found a spot behind, or was it in front of, a bush to go to the toilet. It was a new experience, peeing just exactly where she wanted to, so she relished the moment and added it to her list of growing freedoms.

Revived and ready, Zoe set off again through the dense forest cover, her shoes catching once more in the thorny ground, cracking sticks and scuffing over stones. There was no path here, no one ever came this way and this route belonged only to Zoe. Everybody who swapped the certainty of AarBee to take their chances in the wilderness did so without a path and mostly alone. The faintest whispers of opportunity, folklore and legends were as good as it got. Their destination though, was almost always shared, to the Lifers and to Matthew.

Matthew's legend had grown as powerful as AarBee. He was one of the first to turn away from the promise of immortality, from the seduction of the digital realm. Some said he was a Dupe, kept alive by some program glitch or process error, others that he was born in the wilderness, the child of his mother's rape by thrillseekers. What was beyond doubt though, was that Matthew had taken the myriad of lost Ghosts and wandering apprentices and turned them into Lifers. He had turned loneliness and rejection into a choice, a movement.

Zoe walked all day, stopping occasionally for food or to rest her legs. Sometimes rabbits would wait for her up ahead, before scurrying off as she came close and once, as she sat against a rock late in the afternoon, a young deer wandered elegantly by, tugging leaves from the small trees and listening intently to the breeze.

Zoe travelled for five days like this, just her and the wilderness. As the sun went down she would shake out her sleeping pod and nestle onto the warm ground, her knife in her hand, and in the morning she would rise with the birds and continue her search.

Once, she passed a tiny wooden hut that sat silently in a clearing. She examined it from down on her belly, her eyes peering through the bracken and thorns. It looked in good repair and the clear path that led to the door suggested that somebody lived there, but it was too dangerous to find out who. Zoe didn't need to ask for help and if the house was occupied by Drones, well, that would be that. Besides, there was a faint stench in the air that tasted bad in the back of Zoe's throat and she noticed that the birds didn't sing here, so she crawled quietly away and left the little hut behind.

On the sixth morning, Zoe didn't wake up with the birds. By the time her eyes opened, the full light of the day was streaming through the trees and warming the little sleeping pod. She was tired now, hungry too, her rations were being stretched thinner and thinner and apart from a few berries, she hadn't found anything else to eat. She could have lain on the ground all day, bathing in the forest light and resting her body, but she knew she had to find either food or Lifers, so she dragged herself out, packed her gear away and strode wearily on.

Perhaps she should have knocked at the hut, she thought, taken her chances with the occupants. She had always thought that fate would lead her straight to the Lifers, or that someone would find her as she tramped away from the Metropolis, but at this moment dying alone in the wilderness was looking alarmingly possible. She would have to hunt, she thought, find somewhere to stay for a few days and get her energy back.

As she wandered onwards, adding detail to this thought, the sound of rushing water rose up in the forest. She couldn't place it at first, a mysterious hissing in the distance, but as she came nearer to the source the gurgling and gushing became unmistakable.

The forest floor in front of her dropped away and a gleaming, crystal river came into view. It was a big one, only knee deep, but wide and fast with a waterfall further upstream.

“Fresh water. Maybe fish,” she said to herself, dropping her backpack as she rushed through the fading forest and knelt on the shale bank. She splashed the cool water enthusiastically onto her face, unzipped her utility suit and rolled it down to her waist, scooping the water up under her arms and washing the forest dust from her shoulders and neck.

The water felt good, it danced over her skin in icy blasts and turned her hair to dripping icicles, jolting her senses back to life. She cupped her hands and drank a little, tasting the forest minerals that ran over her lips and down her throat, holding still periodically as she savoured the moment.

"Oh yeah, what have we here??" a voice suddenly came from behind her, making Zoe spin round instinctively.

A young man was leaning against a nearby tree, his arms lolling over the rifle slung across his chest. A second man, a little older but dressed in an identical survival suit and coat, stepped out from the forest cover just behind him.

"Well, you don't get much luckier than that," the older man said, taking a few steps towards Zoe, "not you though sweetheart." He smiled sarcastically.

Zoe sat frozen on the bank, her hands had moved instinctively to cover her chest and water now puddled on her collarbone and between her fingers. She looked around frantically for her rucksack.

"Looking for this?" asked the older man, dangling her rucksack by his side, "Don't worry, you can have it back in a minute."

Zoe wanted to say something but had no idea what to say, she felt helpless and alone with nowhere to run. She leapt up and made a dash for the trees further down the bank, but the younger man had anticipated her escape and within two bounds had his arms around her waist. She struggled with all the strength she had, clawing at his arms and kicking at his shins.

The young man yelped when her heel caught his shinbone with full force and threw her onto the ground.

“Enough!” he yelled, and used the toe of his boot to deliver a precise kick to Zoe's mouth.

She brought her hand up to her face to protect herself from another blow and looked up at the young man who now towered above her. He lifted his foot for the next assault, but then a strange expression came over his face and for a moment everything stopped. It was quiet. Through the silence, Zoe heard a shrill whistle and thump and the young man let out a long breath, before collapsing on the ground next to her. Two short arrows stuck out from his back.

Zoe glanced across at the older man, who was now hopelessly fumbling with the rifle on his chest, a terrified look on his face. Another whistle, this time the arrow struck him in the throat. The man looked at Zoe for a moment, before his legs folded underneath him and he too crumpled onto the forest floor.

Zoe sat up and tugged her utility suit back up over her shoulders. The forest was quiet apart from her panicked breathing, and she scanned around the trees to look for the archer, waiting for the next whistle and thump that would sound her own end. On the other side of the river, a young woman stood watching her, her bow drawn in her hand. Her hair was tied back away from her face and Zoe could see that she was about the same age as her, maybe a little older.

"You OK?" she called out over the sound of the water.

"Yes, thank you," Zoe called back.

There was a pause between them, perhaps neither of them knew what to say next.

"I'm looking for Matthew," Zoe explained finally, moving onto her knees and zipping up her top.

The girl relaxed her bow and lowered it. With her free hand, she pointed upstream to a white rock that rose in the middle of the racing water. There was a tall man standing on it, he was old like the Ghosts, with long grey hair tied up in a ponytail that snaked down his shoulder and back. He was wearing utility trousers, but had no shirt on and his skin looked like dark leather in the sunlight. On his left side, a tattoo of a large bird ran over his shoulder and down his ribs, its red wings spread out wide and glowing in the light. He smiled at her and gave her the most casual wave, like they were just meeting on the most ordinary of mornings.

Zoe got to her feet and waved back.

Matthew

On the edge of the clearing, next to a large wedge-shaped rock – its edges smoothed from centuries of wind and rain, and the more recent touchings of hands and feet that caressed its cool surface or clambered across it to sit on the large flat top – two Hawthorne bushes twisted and twined about each other. Their scrawny trunks swirled three times around, before energetically lancing this way and that in a thousand bristles that exploded with bright red and rich crimson berries. Matthew had studied their shared existence for hours, one native and one synthesised, marvelling at the closeness of the match, comparing the slightly too red red with the deeper, dirtier crimson as they both danced in the breeze with the blue sky behind them.

He wondered how on earth the modified tree had come to be here. One stray tree in the middle of the whole forest, next to an ordinary rock on the edge of one clearing, very much like all the other clearings. Had it been blown here all these miles by the wind, carried high up on the currents of air between here and the managed savannahs? Had it been dropped carelessly by a bird, or fallen from the pack of some unknown traveller, fifty perhaps sixty years earlier?

As he thought, he tumbled a small pebble over and over the fingers in his right hand. He had done it for as long as he could remember, and although the stones had changed over time, after each one was absentmindedly dropped or left in some forgotten place, the feeling of comfort it gave never left him. Up, flip, tuck and roll under. Up, flip, tuck and roll under. Measuring the tiny variations in touch and temperature as he did so.

Today, the clearing was buzzing with the aftermath of a two-day foraging trip. Sorting, packing and storing, the first preparations for another winter, and of course the excitement about the arrival of the new girl. He swivelled around slightly on his perch and watched her for a while, sitting with Jennifer and telling her story, making friendly and enthusiastic introductions to the rest of the camp as they drifted by. She seemed sweet. So young. They got younger and younger every time. She was, doubtless as useless as all the other fresh arrivals, made naive and helpless by a youth spent wrapped in the contrived liberty of AarBee.

She glanced over to him from time to time and he sensed her desire to meet him and prove her devotion. They all did this. It was flattering but he had never really gotten used to it. For someone living in, and leading, such a close and interdependent community, he wasn't much of a people person. It didn't come naturally to him. He had always felt affectionate and compassionate, he enjoyed being a parent to so many children, but he was always one step away from belonging, like he was watching and feeling from some place beyond himself, some place nobody else could reach. As a result, whilst he knew he was loved and respected by the group, he was aware that the real laughter and foolishness, the camaraderie and love, the embraces and tears, often happened in the places and moments he wasn't part of. There was a disconnectedness, a fundamental loneliness that sat in the shadows of every moment he spent with other people, that only really subsided when he was on his own, out in the wilds, focussed on the mundane and automatic routines of survival.

Deep in this thought, his gaze drifted slowly across the scene. There were so many of them now, perhaps as many as three thousand, based mainly at this camp, but also scattered between the two caves that sat a little further downstream and the tiny outpost in the hills. It worked well like that, people could move about as they pleased, joining the hustle and bustle of the main camp with the cave that reached deep into the hillside, each chamber or recess a meeting place, a classroom, a bakery or a place to sleep, or alternatively heading up to the outpost if they needed a quieter existence. The foraging and small game was good at the main camp. Rabbits, pigeon and river fish were plentiful, and there was easily enough to support and replenish them. But up at the outpost, where the landscape hardened up and the wind nipped at your ears even in summertime, the bigger game roamed freely. Once in a while, residents from the outpost would emerge from the trees with slings and sleds overflowing with deer, hare, wild boar and elk, once even a bear, and the whole group would come together to celebrate and share stories and information well into the night.

Their way of life was a strange mixture of tech and prehistoric. Solar panels placed strategically on hillsides and in the forest canopy provided them with basic power needs for light, hot water and to charge what tech they needed. But most of their days were spent foraging and hunting, working small agricultural plots that were cut discreetly into the forest or in hard-to-find gullies and hilltops.

Life was good, but never easy. Safaris were the biggest threat and Matthew lost more of the group to hunters than to animals or injury. They'd set a few traps on the approaches to the camp, but these would catch rabbits more often than hunters and were hard to keep track of if they set too many. Every once in a while, the sound of a hunter's rifle would crack and echo through the forest, and he and the other Lifers would wait nervously to see who didn't return. Sometimes they found the bodies, sometimes they never did. When the hunters used bows the group would only realise their loss as the night closed in, as they bedded down and someone noticed an empty space, or a child stood waiting at the mouth of the cave for a parent who would never show.

On the occasions when they caught the hunters, waiting terrified in the traps or stumbled upon unexpectedly when their paths crossed on an expedition, their revenge was swift and total, but never joyous.

"Am I disturbing you?"

Matthew jumped out of his daydream to see the new girl standing in front of him, smiling nervously.

"I'm sorry," he said, shaking his head a little to signify his surprise and return to the moment, "I was… Have you been standing there long?"

"No, no," she glanced back at the group she had come from. "Well, only a moment or two. I can go if you're busy."

"Ha!" Matthew smiled at how he must look, sitting alone on a rock, staring intently at a Hawthorne bush. "It's fine. What's your name?"

"It's Zoe."

"Well, it's very nice to meet you, Zoe. I hope your trip to get here wasn't too hard?"

"No, it was OK. The first day was the hardest. After that I found the forest quite tame. I felt like I was just out for a walk, you know?"

"You were lucky you didn't get hunted."

"Yeah, thanks for that, they'd have definitely done me."

Matthew smiled at how quickly she'd relaxed again, at the teenage fearlessness that was now adjusting her stance and creeping back into her voice.

"Anyway, I just wanted to say thanks and hello. Thanks for all this, you don't know how long I've been dreaming about escaping."

"You're very welcome, although you don't really need to thank *me*…" Matthew glanced around the clearing and back to Zoe again. "I'm not sure it's much of an escape, but I hope you're happy here. We're glad to have you. Is Jennifer looking after you?"

"Yeah, she's great!" Zoe looked over to her and on catching her gaze, gave her a little wave.

"Well, it's very nice to meet you, I wanted to say how much I admired you, what you've done here." She blushed a little as Matthew smiled an uncomfortable, wordless thanks.

"I'll leave you alone."

She reached out and shook his hand awkwardly, barely even committing to a shake. Her palm was soft, warm and clammy, it felt like a marshmallow inside his dry and cracked grip and Matthew felt reluctant to let something so delicate go. He looked down at his hand for a moment, then watched it relax and let her free, before she jogged back to Jennifer and whatever work they were doing.

As she ran he watched her half adult, half child body, her half Lifer, half Apprentice clothes, her half best friends, half stranger manner with Jennifer and the others. Another one, he thought. Another one to join their quest for something they couldn't define, to escape from something none of them had actually experienced.

He was the only one now who could remember the first few days, the first time he and eleven others had walked across the clearing and into the cave. They'd all gone now, and it made him feel older, perhaps less connected, every time a new one arrived. When he and the Lifers were all people he knew, people who had shared his life and experiences, who had left AarBee behind when it was still a baby project, he had felt a sense of mission and community. They were linked ideologically, a like-minded group not trying to stay in the past, but opting to follow a different future.

Now though, now the kids that turned up barely spoke the same language as him, their experience was only of a suffocating factory education, designed to get them onto narrow apprenticeships, many of which were pointless, wasting as little time and energy on their physical lives as possible before they finally migrated. Their life was Hollers, sync-ups and status, love and friendship served only as the pre-politics to the afterlife and most were so emotionally stunted that calling them 'Lifers' seemed like a cruel joke.

It wasn't a name he had chosen. 'Lifers' had been given to them, a romantic notion of escape and otherness that built them up to be far more than they actually were. A group of runaways really, apprentice fuck-ups and time-outs, with as many here because

AarBee had cast them off as by wilful design. The needy idealists and convenience rejectors made the group weaker than he liked, sometimes barely holding together when arguments flared or the boredom got too much, but they were still here, after all these years, offering the only real choice outside of AarBee other than living as a Ghost, which was a miserable non-existence.

Perhaps they weren't perfect, but then wasn't that also the point? AarBee's world promised perfection, an immortality where every person, every thought and every event from the earliest recordings of human activity, through the present and far into the future, flowed together in one harmonious swirl of data. Matthew's world wasn't about perfection or understanding, it was about the absolute opposite – the friction and confusion, the boredom and the exhilaration. Even the hunters became a peculiar part of their attraction, where death and uncertainty were as essential as oxygen.

That night a large group gathered together to welcome Zoe and celebrate a good haul from the day's gathering. They drank and ate and danced well into the night, pounding rhythms echoing around the cave and out into the high branches of the waning trees. Matthew drank healthily, drowning the melancholy of the day with liquor and adoration. He danced with Zoe and Jennifer, laughing and spinning in the middle of their newly formed group as their bright smiles and virgin hearts energised and intoxicated him. When he finally went to bed, his heavy head sank deep into the furs and fabrics and sleep span its silk around him before he even knew it was approaching.

In his dreams, when the warmth of the evening had retired and left the clearing with a smokey and deserted languor, he found himself floating uneasily through a lonely half-life, drifting on the slightest current through a never-ending maze of tragedy and pain. In every moment of sleep, he was assaulted by terrors and cruelty, with no escape and no way to close his eyes. Corpses littered every view, the remains of the hungry, the lost, the abused – those left alone to die and those who had cowered together and made only a greater spectacle of death. Children wept, mothers curled around them, fathers stood desolate and helpless as some unseen murderer offered Matthew wave upon wave of death to discover.

By morning, when the first chills of autumn stretched and yawned before the sun pushed them away, his mind was pummelled and exhausted from his dream's onslaught. When he opened his eyes the visions of brutality didn't stop, but instead spilled from them in a disgusting torrent that washed over every space, every bed, every sleeping occupant, augmenting his vision with a new perspective and ensuring that his love affair with humanity, with life and the Lifers was unexpectedly, terminally over.

Foraging

When Zoe awoke, her eyes opened gently in the muted underground light and her focus adjusted to the smoothed rock face just a few feet above her head. It took her a moment to remember where she was, her waking dreams still filled with morning routines from the Metropolis, or more recently the crisp dawn chill that drifted through the woods with the early light. There was a rich, heavy scent in the air, the fleshy musk of sleeping bodies and the sulphurous, aged damp of the cave. It should have been unpleasant, but as she came around to her surroundings the pungent air felt comforting, homely and safe, like waking in a nest or deep inside a hidden burrow.

She pushed her hands behind her head and stared at the space around her and the rock above, a broad smile slowly creeping over her face. Yesterday had been a blur of introductions, inductions and spirit-fuelled celebrations. Today would be her first day as a bona fide Lifer. The real deal, breakfast, lunch and dinner. Her excitement fizzed and fluttered in her chest, a great rush of joy that felt like it would arc out of her in a huge rainbow of happiness, enthusiastically illuminating the still sleeping stillness of the cave. It was all she could do not to squeal and she flexed and curled her toes tightly to let loose at least some of her energy.

She turned her head slowly to one side and peered into the dark to see her sleeping comrades. Some were turned towards her, their vacant faces slack and calm with inactivity. Others were buried somewhere deep in the mess of covers, perhaps a bump or stray body part giving a clue to their identity and orientation. Some of the beds were empty and she noticed that Jennifer's, just three away from hers, was already vacated and made. The layers of blankets and animal hides were arranged meticulously so that each one ended six inches short of the next, creating an intricate banding of textures and tone.

Zoe sat up slowly. She caressed the last residues of sleep from her face with both hands and made a few satisfying scratches on her shoulder tops, up her neck and onto her scalp. There were bits and pieces of debris knotted into her hair. Some were small and gritty and stuck firmly to her skin. Others, like the fragment she teased out along the shafts of her hair with her fingernails, were larger. She loved her new filthiness and spent several minutes satisfyingly picking at the endless treasures from her fringe and around her crown.

When she was done she swung her legs out of the bed and stood up, banging her head on the roof of the cave at the exact moment she remembered it was there. She rubbed the impact swiftly with the flat of her hand until the pain receded. Max, one of the older Lifers she had met last night, had his eyes open now and was watching her motionless from his bed. He smiled and emitted a little laugh at her bump, and for a moment she remembered her newbie status bashfully.

“You alright?” he whispered, his deep voice rumbling like distant thunder.

“Yes, thanks,” she replied softly, her voice croaking a little from the atmosphere. “Where’s the nearest toilet?” she asked after a pause, more for something to say than any dire need.

“Outside of the cave, then follow the rock face around to your right. You can’t miss it.”

“Thanks,” she smiled back as she wrapped a blanket around her shoulders and put her shoes loosely on her feet. Her heels stuck uncomfortably out of the backs and she thought about loosening them to put them on properly, before carrying on anyway, hobbling slightly from the discomfort.

The entrance corridor and the area immediately outside of the cave were people-less, although in the hush Zoe could hear the faint rhythms of conversation coming from the kitchens further inside. She skirted around the rock face as instructed and came upon the toilet block, a little ivy creeping picturesquely over the roof, six roughly assembled wooden doors marking each stall. She had been here last night, she remembered, although it wasn't where she thought it was. She noticed three shower heads mounted on the forest side of the block and tracked their fittings up to the roof, where thermo-plastic tubs collected run-off rainwater from the cliff. She would shower here later, she decided. In the moonlight.

Inside the block was less romantic. Vacant cobwebs in every corner fluttered on the light incoming breeze, which was squeezing through the cracks between the timbers, whilst the smell of composting waste rose up in a warm wave from the smooth circular hole cut into the wooden seat. It wasn't a bad smell, but the knowledge of where it came from made Zoe gag uncontrollably when she thought too long about it.

Names and messages were scratched into every surface, a roll-call of all the people who had called the clearing Home over the years.

A fair number had dates, hearts and tributes next to them. "Never forgotten" and "Still my best girl".

They had clearly all died, but Zoe was shocked to see so many. As she scanned the dug out letters, imagining the hands that had carved them there, she wondered which ones had died peacefully in this beautiful place and which had been victim to some Hunter's quest for experiences.

She scanned them for his name too. She couldn't help it. The notion that her Dad had disappeared to join the Lifers, had filled Zoe with the same passion that was directing her now. The possibility that he had made the same journey and walked even along the same path, had forever smouldered inside her and that thought was now fanned back to life by the oxygen of her arrival here. She had looked for him all day yesterday in the older faces she had been introduced to and the distant profiles that had crossed her gaze from the furthest corners of the clearing. She hadn't found him, but there were thousands of people here and, for now at least, she would continue to wonder.

As she left, she ran her hand over the cuts and scars on the walls, making a mental note to bring her knife here next time and add her own name to the record.

Outside again, she spied Jennifer walking briskly across the clearing and called out to her, before breaking into a lolloping jog to catch up.

“Hey sister,” Jennifer called out with a smile as she approached, “I didn’t think I’d see you up for hours.”

“Yeah, I woke up and just figured I should get up. I wasn’t sure what time it was.”

“I’m going to go out on a foraging party again today. We’re still short of a few things – rowan berries, cobnuts. Wanna come along?”

“Absolutely!” Zoe grinned back, not bothering to hide her enthusiasm.

“Great!” Jennifer leant towards her and picked something out of Zoe’s hair, before smoothing her fringe back down.

“Grab some breakfast from the kitchen and I’ll see you out here in half an hour. You’ve time for a shower if you like.”

She gestured towards the toilet block.

“I’m going to have one tonight,” she explained with a grin, as she automatically ran her fingers back through her fringe a few times, “I think that’d be nice, you know, in the moonlight.”

“Sure. Sounds like a plan,” Jennifer smiled warmly towards her, before drooping her arm on Zoe’s shoulder, “Come on, I might grab a tea with you.”

As they walked back inside, down the long central corridor of the cave that led deep into the hillside, with sleeping chambers, kitchens and endless alcoves splintering off down narrow alleyways that you had to crouch into, or ballooning away from the main drag in great sweeping blisters, Jennifer exchanged nods and smiles with all the other Lifers they passed. Zoe nodded and smiled too, doing her best to remember their names as she did.

In the kitchen, they each grabbed steaming mugs of nettle tea and Zoe took a large slice of soda bread with jam and a handful of unroasted nuts before they occupied a spare table scattered with toast crumbs and the rings of earlier teacups. Jennifer blew it clean with a sweeping puff before roughly wiping the wet patches with a cloth that was hooked on one of the table legs. After a few moments Max came in and Jennifer caught his attention with a short and shrill wolf whistle made with her forefinger and thumb. He turned immediately and instinctively to her, as if it was a language they had practised a thousand times before.

“Good morning again,” he said as sat down next to Zoe, his plate now piled high with bread, fruit and what looked like a very pale cheese. Zoe’s side of the table dropped abruptly when he sat down and her arms reached uncontrollably forwards to counterbalance. She glanced across at Jennifer who was smiling right at her.

Max was a giant dark-haired man with broad shoulders and a full, wiry beard that spun down in great twists from his chin. He was one of the older Lifers, a huge man who had dropped out from Drone training years ago and carried several scars from his messy escape. Zoe had met him last night around the fire. He had been out hunting all day and his huge laugh and mesmerising moon-shaped face had become an unforgettable memory of her first, blurry night in the camp.

“We’re going to go out foraging again. I thought I’d show Zoe the ropes, top up the Cobs and a few bits. Wanna come?”

Jennifer sounded different when she spoke to Max, Zoe thought, more forceful, like a teacher or an instructor at one of the apprentice induction camps.

“I HATE foraging,” Max replied from the side of his mouth, a large chunk of bread occupying the other, “all that scrabbling around in the brambles, it’s much easier to set a few traps.”

He raised his hand in front of his mouth to stop the breadcrumbs that were flying out. “It’s more noble.”

They both laughed at this, Max raising his hand as if it would help him swallow the bread.

"Yeah, yeah," Jennifer rolled her eyes at Zoe, "it'll be fun, come on, you could set a trap or two whilst we're there. It's a beautiful day for it."

Max looked at Zoe and winked, "Sure, why not. Have you ever prepped a rabbit?"

Zoe shook her head.

"Great. Then if we get lucky I'll show you how to do it. There's nothing better than fresh rabbit."

"Right," Jennifer stood up from the table abruptly, "I need to sort a couple of things and check in with Matthew. I'll meet you out front in twenty minutes or so."

She took one more gulp of her tea and headed back out to the corridor, dropping her cup in the washing pile on her way past. Max stood up too, cramming the last piece of bread and cheese into his mouth. He glanced at Zoe self-consciously, realising he now couldn't speak and pointed to the corridor, making little walking fingers with his other hand, before giving Zoe the thumbs up and ruffling her hair. When he was gone, Zoe sat quietly on her own for a moment, staring at her cup of tea, before chuckling to herself at the immense pleasure she was feeling from a simple breakfast and the thought of spending the day foraging with

Jennifer and Max. For a moment, her thoughts flashed back to her last breakfast with Sarah and the memory of her squeezing her tightly when she came in. Her smell of yesterday's perfume and bed covers, her voice still a little croaky from sleep, the music playing in the background. It brought a lump to her throat that she fought hard against, pushing it away with thoughts of the day ahead and a reminder that Sarah was gone now.

Twenty minutes later, after she had cleaned her teeth and made a cursory attempt to make her bed – which she gave up on after her desire to straighten the array of blankets and furs ended up with the bed in a worse state than it was before she started – Zoe was sitting in the middle of the clearing, waiting for Jennifer and Max. The sun reached over the treetops and sent white rays slicing through the leaves and branches, and Zoe closed her eyes and aimed her face towards them. They landed lightly on her with the tenderest touch, warming her skin with an even coating of far away fire and giving rise to a feeling of love inside her that she could have indulged forever more. She was so lost in the moment she hadn't heard Max and Jennifer approach, who now stood watching her bliss in silence, half in humour, half in recognition. Eventually, Max shuffled his feet and his proximity made Zoe open her eyes with a jolt.

"Oh, you're here," Zoe squinted at their silhouettes, "I was just enjoying the sunshine."

“Come on,” Jennifer reached out a hand to help her up, “Best time for foraging is the morning. Let’s get going before the sun gets too hot.”

They set off towards the forest on the opposite side of the clearing from where Zoe had arrived, climbing slightly as they reached the treeline, the ropes and traps on Max’s back knocking a little as they swayed with the rhythm of his steps. They walked for two hours without stopping, sometimes following the faint paths that wove around boulders and giant trees, sometimes wading through the thorny undergrowth and ducking under huge leaves that dripped with an endless sappy ooze. Once, they broke out unexpectedly from the clammy shade of the forest into a tiny clearing, no bigger than a few paces wide, where the sunlight beat hard into the tufty grass and clouds of white seed pods drifted silently in the air like summer snow.

Their pace was fast and Zoe's heart was beating hard in her chest when Jennifer finally suggested they stop for a rest, on a cluster of smooth rocks next to a narrow brook.

“Looking a little flushed there newbie,” Jennifer gave Zoe a firm slap on the back.

“I'm OK, just a little hot,” she said, wafting her vest at her waist.

“You'll get used to it, it does get a little suffocating sometimes, doesn't it?”

She passed Zoe a pouch of water, which she glugged from enthusiastically, ignoring the spills that ran down her chin and neck.

"Not far now," said Max, sitting down next to her. "We'll follow this stream 'til it meets the river. There's a pool there that's great for trout and we can set a few traps around about. Good for swimming too."

"Ah, that sounds good," Zoe lay back onto the rocks. She felt their ancient coolness push into the muscles in her back and stared up at the young leaves silhouetted high above her, that fluttered energetically in the open air. For some reason, her mind wandered back to an argument she and Sarah had had a few months before she left. There had been an apprentice Experience Weekend that Sarah was desperate for her to go on, but she'd flatly refused. She knew it would be full of point scorers, trudging around the pristine ranges to engineer themselves a better future. It was the worst of all worlds, and the last thing she'd ever want to do, but she felt regret now that she hadn't gone, at least to make Sarah happy. It seemed such a trivial concession, two days she could have so easily afforded to lose and such an easy pleasure to have given Sarah, now that she looked back at it from her new life.

As she daydreamed, Max refilled the water pouches from the brook and Jennifer foraged about in amongst the trees and rocks looking for finds. Zoe turned her head to one side and watched her expertly strip some small bush of its berries, before she came close again and ushered her up from her rest.

They followed the brook for another half hour, before finally reaching Max's pool. It swelled silently in a ring of pine trees reflecting the white clouds that drifted above them, with a fringe of shale that crunched under their feet as they stood together on the bank.

"It's beautiful," Zoe whispered, not wanting to disturb the perfect stillness that rested there.

"Swim?"

Max didn't wait for an answer before he dropped his pack and stripped off his vest and trousers, kicking off his boots in a knot of trouser fabric. He strode a few paces into the water, sending ripples out across the pool and making little waves that broke on Zoe's feet, before diving head first into the water and coming up gasping a few seconds later in the very middle.

"Come on!" he called out to them.

"You go," said Jennifer, "I'm going to scout around to see what's about. I might join you in a while."

She unclipped her bow and quiver from her pack and slung them both loosely on her shoulder.

"I'll see if I can spot any deer before Max's yelling frightens them off!"

She winked at Zoe and ducked back into the trees. It was kind of her to mention the deer, but Zoe knew that wasn't all she was scouting for. She'd forgotten all about her encounter with the Hunters when she arrived, and she glanced around the treeline for a moment, her eyes delving into the shadows, before putting the memory out of her mind, stripping off her utility suit and diving into the breathtaking water to join Max.

They played together in the pool until they both began to shiver and Zoe's lips turned a damson blue. They dived to the bottom to look for fish and finds in the weeds and dead branches on the riverbed. They floated on their backs under the overhanging branches by the two tributaries that gurgled in upstream, where water boatmen darted out of their way and butterflies and wasps passed by overhead. In the middle of the pool, Zoe made hopeless attempts to dive from Max's shoulders, and they both laughed uncontrollably as he yelped in mock pain and they both inevitably collapsed spluttering into the water.

As they began to talk of getting out, Max called Zoe over to the far edge of the pool, where the water poured out in a silken curve into the river that carried it away downhill, back into the forest. He pulled himself up onto a rock the sat warming in the sunshine and reached out a hand to lift her up beside him.

"Here," he said, making a circle with his hand above the water, "is the best place to catch perch. Watch."

He slid back into the water and propped himself between the rock and the narrow channel of water.

"Just lay your hand flat on the lip here and wait. They come by all the time and you'll see them clear as day."

They both sat in silence for a few seconds, staring intently at Max's submerged palm. For a moment the stillness returned to the pool and the sounds of treetop birds and buzzing flies amplified and then – just as promised – Zoe spotted the faint outline of a small fish pass over his hand. He raised his arm swiftly but steadily, and when it came clear of the water the little fish, just bigger than his hand, was trapped firmly in his fist.

He turned to her with a big grin on his face.

"Easy," his sense of triumph showing plainly in his eyes, "I need to get my bag. You try," he called, as he bounced off through the shallows towards their discarded clothes and kit, clutching his prize.

Zoe jumped back into the water, the cold biting once more at her groin and tummy and making her gasp a little. She lay back against the rock as Max had done, and uncurled her fingers above the smooth rock at the border of the pool, to lie in wait for the next fish. She only had to wait a few seconds before one came along, but she snatched at it with such panic that it darted away and back into the cover of deeper water. She made the same mistake with the next, and the next, but managed to get the fourth fish a few inches out of the water before its wriggling made her relax her grip and it fell away again. Max was by her side now, watching her silently after placing a small canvas bag on top of the sun rock. She relaxed her shoulders and let out a slow breath as she waited for the next fish. This time she waited until it was almost clear past her hand before bringing her fingers around it and raising her arm in one gentle, determined movement. Clear of the water, she gripped it tightly and turned to Max.

"I got it!" she yelled at him, beaming with excitement and dropping it into the sack he had grabbed hurriedly.

"Well done!" he said, inspecting the fish in the sack. "It's a good one. I'm impressed, I didn't actually think you'd get one. It took me weeks to get the knack."

They carried on fishing together, Max on one side of the funnel and Zoe by the rock, their legs motionless in the water and eyes fixed unblinking on the shadows under the surface, until they'd caught six more. Jennifer was back at the bank by the time Zoe landed the sixth and called over to them.

"Very impressive newbie! It took Max weeks!"

He glanced towards Zoe with a look of unbothered agreement.

"You need to get your traps set Max if you want to catch anything at dusk," Jennifer called again after a slight pause.

"OK!" he called back, before bouncing around Zoe to grab the canvas sack from the rock. He waded back to the shore holding the sack at shoulder height, whilst Zoe swam slowly behind him, rolling once or twice to let the cold water fan out her hair.

On the bank, they dried off and got dressed again, whilst Jennifer sorted through her bag of berries and branches, tossing out the occasional twig and bug.

"Right," said Max, picking up the bag of fish and handing it to Zoe. "Whilst I'm setting the traps, you can gut these."

"Err… I have no idea how to do that." Zoe peered into the sack, which smelt earthy and damp, studying the glistening mass of scales at the bottom.

"No problem," Max reached roughly into the sack and swiftly pulled out one fish, "prepare to learn."

Zoe laughed a little. Max looked like some kind of fucked up magician, or perhaps a tragic schoolteacher freaking out the kids. He took the hunting knife from his pocket, before sloshing the fish in the shallow water for a couple of seconds.

"Blade into the arse," he turned the fish belly up and stuck the point of the knife through its skin, just before the tail. "Then cut gently up to the gills. Fingers in, and scoop."

With that he tipped out a small cluster of red and brown entrails and organs that plopped into the water below.

"Then rinse."

He sloshed the fish in the water again for a few seconds, fingering its now hollow body as he did.

"Easy. Do you have a knife?"

Zoe took the small folded blade from her pocket and opened it out for him to see.

"That'll do. All good?"

"Yes, all good."

"Great." Max ruffled her hair again and gave her a wink, before grabbing his pack and disappearing into the forest. He left so quickly her smile and thank you ended up being delivered to an empty space. As she went to straighten her fringe, she remembered where his fingers had been, so instead dropped her head between her legs and shook it out, before tossing her head back to throw her hair over her shoulders. She pulled one piece towards her nose and smelt it. It smelt of the river.

Jennifer, who was sat at the treeline sorting her haul, laughed at her

"I'm sure it's great for your hair," she laughed again as Zoe laughed with her. "I'm going to make one more trip. There's a tree a little further down that is full of nuts. You OK here?"

"Yeah, no problem. I'll get going with these."

Zoe put the bag down and took out the first fish.

"Great. See you in a bit."

And with that Jennifer was gone, and Zoe was on her own in the forest again. It felt different now, though. Last time she was stood alone like this she was full of uncertainty. Now she felt like she knew exactly where she was. Where she belonged. She had only to call out and her two companions would be there for her. She looked down at the tiny fish in her hand and turned it over with her fingers. It was a beautiful thing. Every bit of it sparkled like a jewel. Even it's lifeless eyes gleamed with a brilliant shimmer and as she turned it, a whole spectrum of colours from emerald to lilac, electric to grey, rippled and pulsed over its skin. She stopped turning and carefully pierced the point of her knife into its soft belly, before sawing carefully up to the fleshy dimple under its jaw. She felt the tiny bones grate against the smooth blade as it travelled. When she had tipped out the guts, she washed it as Max had shown her and inspected its insides. Thin white bones tracked in elegant arcs through the deep maroons and blacks of its flesh. She admired the neatness of her surgery before placing the fish carefully back in the sack and choosing the next.

When Max and Jennifer returned, they spent the rest of the afternoon talking, swimming and sorting through the results of Jennifer's foraging. They swapped stories from their pasts, Max with tales of Drone raids and his escape, Jennifer of her run-ins with Hunters and Zoe talked about Sarah and her Dad.

When the sun had faded, Max went to check his traps in the half-light and returned with five rabbits, two of which he skinned and gutted to show Zoe, before Jennifer stuffed their body cavities with nettles and herbs. They lit a small fire on the edge of the pool, and once the embers were wide enough, Max placed a flat rock on top. They stretched out the rabbits and all of the fish onto this, and every once in a while Jennifer would turn them, tipping a little of the juice from the rabbits over the fish.

When they were cooked, Max pushed the rock from the fire with a heavy branch and cut up the meat with his knife. They ate straight from the stone as the fire grew tall again with fresh wood. Max was right, it was the most delicious food Zoe had ever eaten and she washed it down with a little spirit that Jennifer had magicked up from somewhere in her kit bag.

After they had eaten, Max rolled the rock into the pool and strung up a thin tarpaulin between the low branches on the tree line. They stamped down the ground, removing any rocks and built up a layer of ferns, before tossing a couple of blankets down as bedding and a hide each for covers. They lay down together – Max, then Jennifer, then Zoe, each backing into each other for warmth, adjusting the covers over each of them. Jennifer's bow and quiver were placed just above her head, Max's hunting knife was tucked in his belt and Zoe clutched her folded blade in her hand like a child's comforter. They were all asleep before long, and slept deeply in the quiet and still by the pool.

In the morning they woke early, roused by the noise of the forest at dawn and the cold mist that drifted in silver threads before first light. They packed their gear in virtual silence, folding blankets and stringing rabbits together, submerged in the renewed tranquillity of the pool. Once Max had cleared his night traps they set off home and were back at the clearing long before the sun had brought the colour back to the forest.

Jennifer

After they had dropped their haul and emptied their packs, Zoe disappeared to take her shower and Max went to grab an hour's sleep. Jennifer could never sleep again once she was awake, so she went to get some tea and stopped by at her bunk to change her clothes, which were muddy and thorned from yesterday's foraging.

As she shuffled out of the cave with a thermal blanket tossed around her shoulders, she was surprised to see Matthew already up. He was the only other figure moving about in the oyster shell dawn light, pacing about agitatedly along the treeline at the edge of the clearing. She had seen him like this before, often when food stocks were running low or another Lifer had been taken by the hunters. She knew better than to interrupt him. He was always friendly and courteous, but not when he needed to work things out. He wouldn't shout, but would freeze you out with the shortest of sentences and a dead calm face, making the moment as uncomfortable as possible until you backed away voluntarily.

Jennifer busied herself tidying up cups and discarded clothes from the night before. She straightened the tables and rolled away the stray logs that had clustered in small circles, the place markers of conversations and relationships that had bloomed and dispersed during the course of the long night.

They still had yesterday's haul to finish processing and packing, so she would need to get all of these cleared and straightened before they brought the containers back out. It was always amazing how much random stuff disappeared, inadvertently stored away for months at a time if it just happened to be too close to a pile of waiting winter supplies in the busy few weeks when summer drifted away into the autumn mists.

As she tidied, she glanced regularly in the direction of Matthew's lonely, back and forth thinking. She couldn't help it, her physical body reached out towards him before her will had any chance to block it. It caught her by surprise every time and on each occasion she would admonish herself for her stupid gazing. Folding blankets, piling cups near the kitchen store, kicking ashes back into the epicentre of last night’s fire, she would glance over after every task, making a metronome of moments that counted up the growing buffer of time between the potential life they had together and the lonely reality of her inaction.

She hadn't felt like this when they had first met. She had arrived with her boyfriend Richard and had treated Matthew the same as every other member of the group. She admired him, she recognised his achievements and was perhaps even a little in awe of him, but that was as far as it went. Slowly though, after she and Richard separated and Matthew began to include her more and more in the affairs of the group, something had changed. Perhaps it was because he trusted her, the first person in power to ever give her that, perhaps it was because she had been invited to delve the tiniest fraction deeper into his confidence than the rest of the group, perhaps it was simply that here, deep in these woods, she had changed in every way and had shared that journey with him. It didn't really matter, she knew she loved him deeply and spent every moment either bathing contentedly in his company or agonising in the too shallow moments he offered back.

In the five years that she had been with the group, Jennifer had given over every bit of herself to its demands. She had given up her relationships, her time, her independence, every bit of herself she had willingly subjugated for the good of the group. She had even killed for the group, just like yesterday. When the hunters came to take them, to take him, she never hesitated with her bow and her blade. The Lifers had made her a willing killer and her first victim was the girl she used to be.

Not that she missed her old self for one second. The Jennifer she knew before she had made her run to the Lifers was a lonely, tragic girl. Hopelessly underwhelmed with the choices she was offered, dreading the purgatory of migration and exhausted by her own lack of authenticity. She endured ordinary and undemanding apprenticeships, smiled absently through mundane friendships and wandered despairingly around the plastic streets of the Metropolis, all the while daydreaming along the pathways and escape routes of her own internal fantasies. That the girl would die by her own actions was inevitable, turning to the Lifers just gave her a more social and heroic way to do it.

Richard was the only glimmer of hope she had found in all of her twenty years before coming to the forests. They were about as different as they could be, he was a top-tier coder for AarBee, groomed to step into the role of some of the great code shapers, evangelical when talking about the future of the system and ready, so ready, to take his place in the digital world. But somehow, after they had met on a few socials in the apartment block where they both lived, after they had arranged to meet on the Boulevards to share street food and cruise around the tech stores, after they had had sex in the vast emptiness of the savannahs one summer night, he had fallen in love with her. After that, her emptiness had sucked him slowly away from AarBee, warping his trajectory with a prism of young and breathless emotion, until they eventually disappeared together, no doubt to the confusion and horror of all his friends and family.

He hadn't stayed with her for long. She had known it wouldn't last, even though she'd enjoyed the momentary illusion that it might do. When the day to day reality of life outside of AarBee became clear, when the early showings of her newborn self began to emerge, when the first winter had bitten down unforgivingly on their new existence, he had left. Jennifer had woken up one morning and Richard was gone, slipping quietly away as she slept, vanishing into the forest from which they'd emerged. She had cried, perhaps more for the pathetic inevitability of his leaving than for any real sense of loss. When her crying was done the old

Jennifer was too weak and exhausted to resist and the new She emerged complete, without a struggle.

When the rest of the group rose from their beds, Jennifer was ready for them with task lists and orders of work ready to go. Zoe bounded over to her, full of enthusiasm for her second day and her first opportunity to show her worth. Jennifer liked her, she could see all the same scars in Zoe that she had carried, but somehow Zoe managed to bear them without the weight that had crippled, and still shadowed her. She envied her lightness of being, her contagious enthusiasm and the rich, warm humanity that seemed to puff effortlessly from her in pollinating clouds. She watched her as she worked, laughing with the others and found herself smiling whenever Zoe smiled, little darts of energy that pierced her without effort and burst in tiny explosions in her spirit.

They worked all through the morning, splitting, cleaning, freeze-drying, vacu-packing and synthesising where they could. Nuts and hard fruits synthesised really well, whereas berries and meat were always a disaster. They didn't have the environment free labs you needed for that level of farming, not out here in the wilds.

Later on in the afternoon, as the evening chill just started to tap on their cheeks and fingers, a lone figure appeared at the very edge of the clearing. Zoe had spotted him first, lurking in the cover of the low branches and rocks that furred the divide between bright open space and dark forest. As more and more of the group looked towards him he moved slowly from the shadows with his arms raised at right angles to his body, perhaps fearing he would be shot if he didn't show himself unarmed. He was wearing a migration farm utility suit and Jennifer's first thought was that they were about to be attacked. Nobody ever turned up in uniform, that was always the first thing to get ditched.

As they all stood motionless – the whole work party in frozen silence – Matthew emerged from somewhere beyond Jennifer's gaze and walked slowly towards the visitor. She glanced around in a panic, looking for her bow or a knife, her heart racing with the powerful sense that they were about to be set upon, or Matthew ambushed.

As she stared back at the lone figure, she could see dirt and scuffs on his suit, and as he moved slowly towards Matthew he seemed to be limping. Matthew and the visitor talked for a few moments whilst the gentle breeze sent the early autumn leaves fluttering softly around them, animating the portent of the moment that burned hot in Jennifer's muscles and sinews. When Matthew took the visitor's hands in his, it looked for a moment like a far away wedding, made serene by the fading light and the buzz in her ears. Eventually, Matthew and the visitor turned to the group and walked towards them, Matthew supporting the man's weight by his elbow.

"This is David," Matthew called out loudly, still holding on to his arm, "he was attacked at Beta Farm by a large group of Drones. He says all of the apprentices and Migrants were killed."

Matthew let his news hang in the air and moved his gaze slowly across the group, as if he was measuring their response. The silence kept its firm grip on the moment, letting the cold breeze mark time with regular pulses in their ears.

"Why?" Jennifer finally called out, having churned the question around her own mind since Matthew spoke.

"I don't know," David answered meekly. "There was no warning, no reason, they just arrived."

"AarBee!" Matthew spoke forcefully to him, nodding out to the rest of the group watching.

"Maybe, they didn't say anything, just started shooting…"

"Of course it's AarBee. There's no way anybody else could use the Drones." Matthew snapped a little, then patted the air with his hands to calm himself down as they reached the group, "Was there a plot, a demonstration?"

"No, nothing. Well not that I knew of. It was just a regular day…" David drifted away for a moment, as if the scene was playing over again, just beneath the surface of his skin.

He looked up at the group, who all stood silently watching him, "Is there some food? I'm sorry but I haven't eaten since I left."

"Yes, yes, I'm sorry," Matthew took his arm again, "Jennifer, could you look after David, perhaps find him somewhere to rest."

Jennifer stepped towards him and smiled, although her uncertainty and distrust was so in control of her face that only she knew there was a smile there. Now she was closer to him she could see he was only a young man, his boyish face perched awkwardly on top of a muscular adult body. Fear and exhaustion were everywhere about him. His hands were shaking and although he tried to hide his eyes with a downward, submissive stoop, there was so much terror in them that he looked like he would cry at any moment. She had seen this look before, in the hunters that she had killed and on the faces of her Lifer friends in the last moments before they slipped from living to permanent death.

"Come on," she said, her voice quieted by questions, before leading the way to the cave to feed him and find him somewhere to sleep. She grabbed a handful of berries from a container on the way past, which she dumped unceremoniously into his hands and he crammed into his mouth with a similar lack of ceremony. She took him to her bed, it was easier than searching for a spare bunk further inside the cave and found him some grilled meat rations that he devoured with a grotesque enthusiasm. He was clearly telling the truth about not having eaten.

Once he was fed she encouraged him to lie down, which he did in a kind of wide-eyed stupor before falling asleep, to her amazement, in ten seconds flat. She stared at his sleeping face for a while, streaked with dirt and berry juice, but wiped clear of the fear that had distorted and aged it just a few moments earlier. He was well looked after, protected and loved. There was no loneliness or hopelessness scribed into his skin. The trauma from the last few days had lifted almost instantly, although Jennifer knew it would settle back down upon him in some way or another, eventually putting its mark on his smooth black skin and burrowing deep into his organs.

She headed back out into the clearing, where the group buzzed with speculation as to what was happening in the Metropolis. Matthew was talking with a small group on the far side of the clearing, his arms waving animatedly about with a wild and twitchy passion. Zoe rushed over to her.

"That must have been the day after I left!" she said with an excited horror, "I was at Echo Farm with my Mum just the day before!"

"He's Beta," said Jennifer, "I doubt anything happened at Echo, they're miles apart."

"Yes but, you know, it could've been me. It could have been us!" Zoe stared intently at Jennifer, looking for reassurance and perhaps someone to revel romantically in her near miss, at least for a moment, but Jennifer wouldn't be drawn.

"What do you think happened?" Zoe relented after a while.

"I don't know, and I can't say I really care. What happens in the Metropolis doesn't interest me, as long as they stay far away from here. They can all kill each other for all I care. Oh wait, they already do." Jennifer gave Zoe an exasperated curl of the lip, and Zoe returned a look of shock at her coldness.

"I was only there last week," she said sharply, "it's different for me."

There was a brief pause between them that Jennifer was about to fill with an apology, conscious of the coldness of her response and just how far she'd drifted from the girl-like-Zoe she used to be, when their attention was taken by calls from the group as they all turned to look again towards the forest. Standing at the treeline were a man and woman, clearly older this time, but both in Farm utility suits. The bright red trim of their uniform etching them out against the darkening foliage that swayed and hissed behind them.

"Delta," said Zoe in a stunned whisper.

"Shit," Jennifer answered.

They welcomed these two into the clearing, just as they had welcomed the boy, hearing first their story of murderous Drones, out of control killing sprees and how they were the only few who had escaped, before they fed them and offered them somewhere to rest. Night was coming, the skies swirling with cloud and darkening into thick ochre ribbons high above the forest that reached all the way back to the wall and the savannahs beyond.

In the hour or so before darkness finally shut down the possibility of navigating the dense and rocky woodland trails, at least without the risk of breaking an ankle or walking obliviously into the black plummet of a ravine, another six travellers turned up. Four arrived in one group, senior administrators from Beta. They knew David and were relieved and surprised to hear he had reached the camp. The other two arrived independently, a young man who cleaned the Vactrains that serviced Delta and an older woman in her late-twenties who had fled from the terminal at Beta when the Drones began firing.

She had been due to migrate that day, and had set off to the Farm with her younger sister for company. She described how everything was normal when they pulled into the terminal. She had been talking to her father who had hollered with them for the journey, the doors had opened and everyone had begun to exit when the Hollers suddenly vanished. The Drones on the platform, who had been helping and talking only moments before, simply raised their weapons and began to fire into the crowds. She and her sister had seen hundreds fall. They had escaped only because the doors had failed to open on their compartment as they were too far down the platform.

As they watched through the refracted glass of the door, people had simply stood frozen to the spot, not understanding what was happening, assuming perhaps that this was happening around them and not to them. Others had tried to run but had been picked off as they crossed the wide-open lawns and concourse. As more Drones poured out of the Farm, the stragglers and the wounded had been killed without hesitation, but not the young children. She remembered seeing the children standing in small clusters as the slaughter happened around them, herded together or crouched alone on the floor.

Whilst the Drones were busy killing, she and her sister had escaped from a fire window at the rear of their compartment, crawling along the tube before exiting via a maintenance hatch and slipping into the undergrowth, before finally heading out across the savannahs towards the wall and the forest beyond.

She wept uncontrollably as she recounted how she had left her sister at the wall, a deep cut along her leg sustained as she fell from the train finally making her immobile, fate refusing to let her run out on her life with AarBee. She had left her propped against the wall with water and chocolate to make her comfortable, her skin turning as grey as stone, her fading eyes keeping watch across the wide savannah with a whistle to blow if she saw Drones approaching, or other survivors who could help.

Refugees

The camp was up late again that night, though not with the music and laughter of the night before. This time, a sombre mood mingled with the night air and woodsmoke. Small groups sat around the fires that dotted the clearing like beacons, whilst others came together around tables or curled up on rugs in the warm chambers deep in the cave. Some spat angry words and punched out violent gestures that cast long and haunting shadows into the trees or across the cave walls. Others talked in hushed and secretive tones, frightened and timid nocturnal creatures with one ear scanning the forests from a fear that couldn't be placated. The rest sat quietly, with heads on shoulders and hands being held. Hair was smoothed gently from forehead to neck, as they thought of their loved ones who remained in the Metropolis or mourned helplessly in the tragedy of the loss of so many strangers.

As the night deepened, the murmur of voices faded along with the dimming fires left unattended once everything that could be said had been shared. The cave that had been home to the Lifers since Matthew's first steps inside it, wrapped gently around the group as one by one they settled into sleep, soothed by a lullaby of distant sobs that moved through the cave like a yawn before finally petering out. Every now and then David would shout out in his sleep, haunted by the faces of death and oblivion, and Jennifer would put her arm across him, letting the weight of her bones push him back to safety.

In the early morning, when troubled thoughts and endless circling questions forced Jennifer and a few others out of sleep, it was raining hard. They stood together in silence at the mouth of the cave, watching the water pummel the earth and bounce in countless tiny explosions off the rocks and stray possessions that lay randomly around the clearing. There would be little they could do today until the downpour passed, there would be no escape from the heavy gloom that glued them together in that space, until the rain let them out.

They ate breakfast and drank nettle tea there, the group growing by one or two every few minutes. Chairs were carried over, then a few tables with more food, blankets on knees, coffee, somebody even played some music. They sat there together for over an hour, a surprise audience in an enormous theatre, watching the morning perform a slow and meditative drama of light, movement and sound. Leaves shuddered and shimmered under the downpour, glimpses of muted daylight made the air roll through sharp and crystal vanillas to deep and dark mossy greens, and when the wind rushed across the clearing the rain clustered into giant chandeliers that swept across their view and down into the trees. Nobody spoke during their time in the mouth of the cave, there was no talking to be done. Soon though, they began to make little jokes with one another, stupid faces and childish games until smiles and giggles began to grow and the whole group was laughing hysterically together at the ridiculous moment they had made. Jennifer laughed too, an uncontrollable but silent belly laugh that she couldn't remember ever having done before, that made tears run down her cheeks and her ribs ache as if she had been punched. Other members of the group, awake now and puzzled by this bizarre scene approached them with confused expressions, smiling a little to join the fun, and that's when someone noticed Matthew. He was standing on the far side of the clearing, almost disappeared into the trees with his back to the cave, his arms clenched tightly to his chest, stamping his feet a little as if he was marching on the spot. The laughter stopped and a long awkward silence took its place.

"What's he doing?" someone finally asked.

They all looked at Jennifer.

"He goes there to think," she said, trying not to show her concern.

"In the pouring rain?" someone else came back. "Why is he standing like that?"

"He's fine!" she snapped. "I'll go talk to him."

Jennifer stood up from her chair and tucked it back against the cave wall. She wiped a remaining tear from her cheek and looked around for a raincoat to borrow.

"Look!" someone called out.

Jennifer turned expecting to see the group staring at Matthew, but instead they were now looking back to the other side of the clearing. Emerging from the trees was another group of refugees, a huge group this time, fifty, maybe sixty. There were young children with them, babes in arms and a couple of people on makeshift stretchers that were now propped awkwardly on the rocks.

"I'll go get Matthew," Jennifer said to nobody in particular. "You go and find out who they are."

With that, she raced into the rain without a coat towards Matthew who was still standing as he was, with his back to the unfolding events. As she ran towards him, she called his name into the driving rain, but he didn't respond. She slowed her run as she came closer, dropping to a cautious approach when she came up alongside him. He was soaked through, his long grey hair funnelling water down his back and his clothes sticking to him like thin layers of latex. His head was dropped strangely low onto his chest and he seemed to be staring intently at his fingers, which twitched and fidgeted rapidly just above his stomach. His lips were moving equally fast, but she couldn't hear his words.

She called out his name twice and when she touched him on the shoulder he finally acknowledged her, not with a start, but instead with a strange, defeated smile she had never seen him give before, as his hands fell slowly back down to his side.

“Hello Eve,” he said in the most normal of voices.

“It’s Jennifer, Matthew,” she touched him again on the shoulder, feeling his heavy bones sticking up sharply from the wet skin and cloth that was draped over him. He looked so much older all of a sudden, she had never paid it much notice before. But now, soaked through and smiling gently in the rain, still hunched over slightly with the faintest trace of confusion in his eyes, he looked like a lost and lonely old man.

“Who’s Eve?” she asked, the rain beginning to pool and flood across her own face.

“Sorry, how stupid of me,” he said, shaking his head, his face firming up again as he spoke the words, his body reforming into the Matthew she knew better.

“It’s raining.” Jennifer raised her palms up towards the thick and dark clouds that sprawled above their heads. She smiled back at him, bundling all her fear, bemusement and love into just one tiny configuration of the muscles in her face.

“Yes, it’s beautiful isn't it, I wanted to feel it, to experience it.”

“Well, you’ve certainly done that,” she said, casting an eye over his soaked clothes. “More refugees have arrived, too many. Look.”

Jennifer pointed towards the opposite side of the clearing, where by now a number of Lifers had reached the large group and were leading them towards the cave. It was a pitiful sight, a random collection of Metropolitans, some in raincoats and boots, others seemingly in the clothes they wore in their apartments. Their utility suits had insignias on them, a few were from Farms, some seemed to be from the Server and Municipal teams. One girl was still wearing her restaurant uniform, her apron now tied around her head like a baby's bonnet. It looked like a failed recruitment parade, made ludicrous and tragic by the rain and hasty organisation.

The rustle of leaves and the sudden crack of a branch underfoot made them both start, and they turned back sharply towards the tree line behind them. In amongst the trees, cowering a little, with rain streaming down his short dark hair and sodden clothes, a young boy stared back towards them, his left hand outstretched as if to defend himself from a blow. Jennifer instinctively put herself between Matthew and the boy.

"Stop there," Jennifer shouted at him, reaching down to grab a heavy branch she'd spied at the foot of one of the Oak trees, her eyes fixed on him.

"I'm unarmed," he called back, raising both his arms to demonstrate, "I'm just looking for shelter."

"It's alright," said Matthew, putting a hand on Jennifer's shoulder and stepping around her.

"It's OK, I'm sorry, we're not used to so many arrivals."

Matthew took a step towards him and beckoned him out of the trees.

“Where are you from?”

“Prime Code,” he glanced at his uniform as he said it, as if it should be obvious to them.

“And why are you here?” Jennifer asked bluntly.

“We were monitoring some weird power surges and data shifts in the system, when… well, we just couldn’t work it out, it went crazy, you know? Systems offline, lock-outs, corrupt chains, glitches all over the place. Everybody went nuts trying to stop it.”

He spotted the group of travellers on the other side of the clearing and pointed towards them, “They’ll be a lot more, it’s all gone crazy.”

“It’s OK, you’re safe here,” Matthew smiled at him and flicked his eyes from Jennifer to the group in the clearing.

“We need to get them inside and warm,” he said, the authority spreading across his face again, filling Jennifer with a comfortable emotion that she had only noticed she carried when it had temporarily faded moments earlier.

Jennifer nodded and turned to head back towards the cave.

“Wait!” the boy called out. “There’s something else, something I found before the power went off. Someone here.”

There was a pause as they both stared at the boy.

"I'm not sure," he carried on awkwardly, looking at Jennifer now, "I might be wrong, it just seemed like…"

"Wait. Jennifer, you need to deal with them," Matthew cut him off, glancing again towards the large group who were now stretching right across the clearing and crowding around the cave entrance. "I'll talk to…" Matthew raised his pitch into a question.

"Cain," the boy replied.

"Cain," Matthew repeated.

When Jennifer got back to the cave she could see that the group in the entrance were still watching Matthew closely. They hadn't seen the frail old man she had met, thankfully Matthew had re-buried him, but they were still puzzled, perhaps a little frightened by his behaviour. Matthew was always so solid, so perfect, so justified, a voice of reason, calm and hope that they all leant on in some way or another. They owed him everything and even in their darkest times of crisis or confrontation never questioned his status at the head of the group, but now, perhaps, something irreversible had happened that would make their confidence in his authority waver.

***

That day, the whole group shifted automatically, almost without any conferring or questions, into the role of carer and redeemer of the Metropolis. No one could have ever imagined that they would be called upon to care for the people they had run from days, weeks and years earlier, to offer shelter and sanctuary to the privilege and security they had rejected so completely, but they adapted to it as if it had always been the plan.

The rain ran heavy from the morning into the afternoon, refusing to yield as the humble daylight waned and the evening's shade drifted wet and dejected into the clearing. With every sheet of rain and blast of the needle-filled wind came yet more refugees, shivering and crying out from the sodden forest into the arms of the Lifers.

Without question, but with a clear understanding of the consequences, the winter provisions so carefully packed away over the past few days were re-opened and offered up to the crisis. Long held stores of dried meat and preserves were gifted, blankets were shared and every spare space was given over to the refugees. Hundreds of them arrived over the course of the day, each with their own story but all telling the same tale. AarBee had turned on the Metropolis, the power had gone out, food had run out and the Drones had slaughtered at will and at random.

The shock of the situation was everywhere. Lifers and refugees alike sobbed and collapsed whenever and wherever the scale of events became too much to bear – while tales were being told, when news of loved ones came, as wounds were dressed, food given out, or in those brief moments alone that could be deliberately found or accidentally stumbled upon.

Everybody dealt with the day's events in their own way. Some found comfort in the large groups that managed the issue of fresh clothes and finding a bed, others flitted from place to place, helping here and there with a restless energy that refused to let reality settle upon them. A few, like Jennifer and Matthew, brought up the barriers that were always there, to keep the world away from the last remnants of themselves that lay hidden somewhere deep inside. Moving coldly and efficiently through the present, being strong, keeping it together, they sent their emotions off to join the other ghosts and spectres that would shred them discreetly when they slept, bubbling undercurrents that twisted and tore relentlessly beneath the smooth and still layers of skin.

After dark the torrent of new arrivals finally slowed and stopped, the forest claiming any more wanderers as its reluctant guests, at least for one more night in the cold cover of the canopy. Inside the cave activity began to slow as the last arrivals were fed and found a place to sleep. With this new calm, Matthew sent word for all the Lifers to come together in the meeting chamber and slowly, exhaustedly they filtered in until the huge, vaulted space was packed full. When the last few had arrived, bloodied and drained from the makeshift hospital, Matthew dragged a chair into the middle of the room and stood up on it to address them all.

"I want to thank you, thank all of you, for what you have done today," he turned slowly on the chair to acknowledge every angle. "I know today has been hard, I know we have made some difficult choices, but I have never been more proud of you, of us."

Every face in the room was fixed upon him. Some smiled back at him, a gentle acknowledgement of their comradeship, a few tears ran down faces still raw with the emotion of the day. They all knew the choices he was referring to, they all knew that everything had changed in just 12 hours, that if the refugees were here then AarBee must surely be set to follow. That no matter what happened, they could not now survive the winter in the Outland Forest.

"We have to go to the Metropolis."

There was a collective gasp, followed by a buzz of chatter that grew louder and louder. Matthew put his arms out to calm the room.

"That'll be suicide!" somebody called out.

"Our supplies are gone!" Matthew called back, beckoning the room quiet again and waiting until they finally settled.

"Our supplies are gone. AarBee may well be coming here and besides, if it's true about the children being taken, we can't leave them. I don't see that we have a choice."

On the other side of the room, Jennifer appeared above the crowd, raised up on the stone steps that jutted out from the far wall, the minerals in the rock glinting slightly behind her.

“Matthew is right,” she called out defiantly to the room, “if we stay here we’ll all starve. There’s not enough for us, never mind our guests. And how many more are coming?? If we do nothing, we’re dead.”

The room watched her silently.

“We’ll go tomorrow,” Matthew spoke again, “I want a small group to head up to the Outpost and let them know. Max, you’ll organise this please. You’ll stay there and help increase the hunting yield.”

He looked across at Max who nodded slowly back, both hands wrapped tightly around his teacup.

“We’ll make for Echo Farm, it's closest to us. I need volunteers for the raid, our hunters and those with skills from AarBee, the rest can stay here to keep the camp running and look after our guests.”

With that, Matthew stepped down and the chatter buzzed back up in the room again as the Lifers talked excitedly about the plan, and what tomorrow would bring.

The Raid

Zoe couldn't believe that only two days after finding her way to the Lifers, she was heading back to the Metropolis. The blisters on her feet were only just drying out, the pain in her muscles had only just begun to ease off and she had barely even begun to feel that her life with them might be a reality. She had hardly had the chance to feel homesick, to crave toast and pancakes, to dream of a Sunday spent gaming with Sarah, to miss the boulevards and tech stores. She could still smell the Vactrain on her clothes. Worst of all, she knew that some of her friends wouldn't have known that she had even gone yet. Her personal rebellion, her singular leap from AarBee into the unknown, would be lost in the crowds of refugees and clouds of turmoil that were now the norm.

After Matthew's announcement the night before, she and a few others – old hands and newer arrivals – had talked long into the night about the raid. Although nobody came right out and said it, they all shared their fear and uncertainty, secretly bundled up with their annoyance at the inconvenient arrival of the refugees, the arguments about the best way back to the Metropolis and the bravado of how to kill. Apparently, there was a secret way back that only Matthew knew about. This would spare them the four or five-day journey through the forest and instead get them there in a day, if they walked at speed. Zoe was happy about that. Although she had enjoyed her solo wander through the maze of trees and thickets and hidden streams, her feet still felt swollen and sore, and the need to climb back into her travel pod in this weather was one she'd avoid at any cost. The rain would surely pile on the discomfort, even during the shorter journey, but her outdoor gear was almost new and she could deal with the wet weather if she was zipped and clipped up.

Yesterday's downpour had continued relentlessly through the night and was still drumming down in the clearing this morning. Zoe shuffled silently over to the cave entrance, picking up a mug of chocolate as she passed the kitchen and wrapping her fingers tightly around its warm curves, before staring out at the waterlogged scene. The sky was brighter today, with slim peels of lemon and crystal light cutting through the deep grey cover. Zoe thought the rain might even be slightly lighter, although she wasn't sure whether she was just being optimistic.

She glanced to her left, following the trees as they climbed gently away towards the distant mountains, and spotted a dozen or so tiny figures shrinking with distance on the dark brown forest path as it cut in and out of the emerald and black hillside. Max must have gotten away early. She wondered who had gone with him and strained her eyes to make out some recognisable features on the silhouettes as they moved at speed along the track. But they were already too far in the distance to give themselves away. She marvelled at how fast they were moving, almost sprinting away from her, crouched down low and moving like a pack, before they disappeared into the deep and dense foliage that swallowed the path for good.

She wished he had picked her for the trek up to the Outpost, and thought how exciting it would have been to be running with them through the forest, carrying just enough provisions to get there, foraging what they could along the way. It was exactly what she had dreamed of from the safety and comfort of her bed back in the Metropolis. For a moment, she was tempted to grab her things and race off after them, but she thought better of it, she would never catch them now and didn't want the rest of the group to think she was running away from their march to Echo Farm.

As she stared up at the distant mountains, lost in her thoughts of wild freedom and camaraderie, she forgot about the hot chocolate in her hands and it fell suddenly with a crack onto the floor, spraying chocolate onto her feet and legs as it did.

"Clumsy," came a voice from behind her. It was Jennifer, already dressed with an open pack slung untidily across one shoulder.

"I hope you're better with a gun, otherwise we'll all be dead before we get there."

"Bloody chocolate everywhere," Zoe said, brushing her legs down and picking up the two perfect half-mugs. She looked up at Jennifer and saw that her clothes were patched and dotted from the rain.

“You’re wet,” she frowned and tilted her head, “out already?”

“The boy from yesterday. Max found him in the willow tree by the river. Hanged himself. I had to cut him down.”

“Oh no, that’s sad, he'd only just got here.” Zoe felt her words sounded foolish, a little empty, and gazed back out across the clearing to hide her awkwardness. She thought she should have felt sadder about it than she did, but with everything else that was happening it seemed a disrespectfully minor piece of news.

“I saw Max and the Outpost group, I think.” Zoe pointed up to the rising forest.

“Quick aren't they!” Jennifer smiled.

“Like crazy. I wish I was going with them, really.”

“What and miss all the fun at the Farm? You'd regret it. Besides, I kind of want you there, I think you'll be handy.”

Zoe smiled at Jennifer, she knew she didn't really mean that, but it was nice that she’d even bothered to say it. Perhaps she was right, perhaps going up to the Outpost would be missing out, perhaps she owed it to everybody to prove herself at the Farm. Her heart beat a little faster at that thought and butterflies flew briefly around her neck and middle. She had been brought up to fear and steer clear of the Drones, so going back to the Metropolis on a raid guaranteed to result in a fight with them sat uneasily in her thoughts.

“Hello?” Jennifer's voice jumped Zoe back from her daydream again, “Blimey, don't you start being weird as well, enough of that going on already! Come on, you need to eat some breakfast.”

With that Jennifer grabbed her hand and pulled her towards her, wrapping an arm tightly around her neck and leading her almost bent double towards the kitchens.

The enormous chamber was buzzing. The Lifers going on the raid were all up and dressed in all-weather suits, with packs scattered around the floor and hung up on chair backs and hooks in the walls. Here and there, small groups of refugees sat together, picking at breakfast and drinking tea whilst trying to have a conversation over the huge noise of excited chatter and clattering plates that reverberated around the hall.

Zoe and Jennifer queued briefly at the service counter, with Jennifer’s arm still limply slung around Zoe’s neck, and picked out eggs, toast, berries and great mugs of steaming tea to fuel them for their trip. Jennifer picked out a couple of extra hard-boiled eggs and some toast and shoved them into Zoe’s pockets.

“You’ll be glad you’ve got these later, when all the greedy bastards eat everything else!” she laughed.

They shuffled on to the end of one of the long tables and tucked into their food, joining in the loud and cheerful conversations that bounced up and down the rows of laughing faces, eating frantically. Zoe watched for a minute and was struck by how animated and happy everybody now seemed. It wasn't that she had found the Lifers unfriendly or downcast in the first place, they had welcomed her with open arms and had become like family almost immediately, but something had definitely changed in the last 24 hours. This morning felt more like a birthday party than the eve of conflict. It was as if the previous day's events hadn't occurred at all, or they had been joined by long-lost family, rather than hordes of strangers. Perhaps, after so long seeing themselves as the outsiders, the renegades who ran away from the world, they had suddenly been presented with the opportunity to be heroes, saviours of the people, and they were all ignited and united by their new-found status.

They sat together like this for almost an hour, sharing stories and silly jokes, eating their fill and, for Zoe at least, drinking way too much tea. Her heart raced and her mind jittered, sped along by whatever stimulant was contained in the foraged Lifers' blend tea. When Matthew appeared at the entrance, the room slowly fell to a hush and all heads turned towards him.

"We need to go," he said in a gentle voice.

After the slightest pause, which allowed his words to hold grandly in the moment, chairs grated back and plates were hurriedly stacked as the group made ready for their long march. There were hugs and slaps on the back, kisses and smiles, but no tears.

Zoe had no one to say goodbye to. Her Lifer friends were all going with her. So, once they were out of the kitchen she took her coat and pack from her bed, zipped herself in and tightened the straps around her shoulders. Jennifer disappeared briefly and returned carrying her bow and a short, stubby gun.

"This is for you," she said, holding it out to her with one outstretched arm, "don't put your finger on the trigger until you need to."

Zoe took it from her and looked at it cradled in her hands. It was lighter than she thought it would be.

"Here," said Jennifer, slinging the strap around her neck and adjusting it so it hung across her middle with the muzzle pointing to the ground. "Well, you look the part and that's half the battle!"

Jennifer eyed her like a proud mother on the first day of an apprenticeship and then turned around to head for the mouth of the cave. Zoe followed just behind her and when they joined the others outside in the morning air, their march to the Metropolis began.

They talked enthusiastically at first, the rain clattering down through the leaves and onto their hats and coats as they walked three or four abreast through the forest. They walked on a well-worn path for the first mile or so, but then cut down a steep ravine and picked up an almost invisible animal trail that descended gently downwards. Oaks and beech trees gave way to rigid lines of pine, a sweet smelling memory of a managed past that was now wrapped in the reckless twines of rhododendron and bramble. Here they moved to single file to avoid the relentless tripping and snagging that was inevitable when stepping even slightly away from the laser thin path. As their heads dropped to watch their feet, so too the conversation fell away and they walked in a collective silence to the rhythm of their pace and the constant rain.

After three hours of almost continual descent, they finally broke clear of the trees and came upon an old steel railway track that cut a deep path between the forest and a bleak and rocky bluff on the other side.

“We’ll rest here for a few minutes,” Matthew called out after scrambling a few feet up the rocks opposite. “Drink some water, eat some food. These tracks will take us all the way to the Farm, we won’t stop now until we’re there.”

Zoe dropped her pack and gun, which had been cramping into her shoulder muscles almost since they left, and rocked her arms backwards and forwards with a bliss and lightness that made her head feel as if it was about to float right off her neck. She sat down on a dry looking patch of moss, with a curved rock to cradle her back and loosened her boots slightly. When her muscles were recovered she reached into her pack and pulled out her water bottle, bread and preserved meat and began to tuck into them hungrily.

After a few minutes, Jennifer arrived and sat down next to her.

"How you doing?"

"I'm good. Starving!" Zoe said still chewing on a large mouthful of bread.

"Make sure you save a little for later. We might have to wait it out depending on what time we get there."

"Sure. What is this railway?" Zoe nodded down at the rusted steel track as she asked.

"Apparently, it's an old freight route that used to link the Metropolis to some quarry or something. Years ago we're talking. It's all forgotten about now, hasn't been used since before AarBee. It's the route that Matthew used to escape, before he found the cave."

"Wow, he was lucky," Zoe smiled, "five days in the forest for the rest of us!"

"I know, right?!" Jennifer leant forward and stroked her hand back and forth on the coarse and rusty steel track. "I wonder how far it is?"

"To Echo?"

"No, to the quarry." Jennifer brought her head down to rest on her hand and gazed down the track as if she was lining up a gun sight. "I'd like to have been a miner. All dynamite and cranes and loading freight trains. I'd eat my lunch sitting on top of a huge boulder and wash the dust off every night in a steaming hot shower. I'll bet it's beautiful there now, all overgrown and silent."

"We should go there," said Zoe, "when we get back."

Jennifer glanced up at her with a gentle, dreamer's smile. "Yes, I'd like that."

"OK, let's go!" Matthew's voice called out from up ahead, and everybody got to their feet and slung their packs back on. Zoe crammed another chunk of bread into her mouth and took a swig of water to chew it with. The dough pulped up in her mouth, and when she swallowed it tracked slowly down her throat like it was triple the size. She swallowed hard to force it down and hoped Jennifer wouldn't notice her eyes watering.

They trekked along the train tracks for the rest of the day, the loose stones and industrial gravel taking its toll on their feet and ankles. The rain continued without a pause, but in the shelter of the deep cut of the tracks it was easy to ignore. Many of them chose to drop their hoods, opting to get wet but talk easily instead of sheltering in the muffled, half-blind fabric curves. The track was wide and flat, so they moved in big billowing groups now, rather than the narrow line from before. It was more sociable that way and the conversation was so relaxed and easy, Zoe had to keep reminding herself of the purpose of their march. Each time she thought about it, her grip would tighten on the handle of her gun, her jaw clench a little and her heart rush just a little higher in her chest.

As the daylight began to fade slightly, the red-tipped tower of Echo Farm finally came into view, a thin white shard that rose sharp and unforgiving on the very edge of the grey haze of the horizon. Matthew and the others at the front of the group stopped and as they all bunched up they acknowledged its appearance with a contemplative silence. The lights from the small cluster of buildings below it shone brighter than Zoe had expected, it must be darker and later than she thought.

“There are no lights on in the Metropolis,” someone called out.

Zoe scanned up to the spaces far beyond the Farm. She could just make out the gentle edges of a few apartment blocks standing above the rained out low-rise buildings that sprawled away towards another faint red beacon in the distance, which must be Delta or perhaps Beta Farm, but there were no lights on anywhere. It was a curiously haunting view, utterly still and almost hand drawn behind the constant veil of rain.

“We’ll head down until we reach an old signal point,” Matthew called back. “Once we’re there we’ll wait till it’s dark and drop down off the track. We’ll go the rest of the way through the parks.”

They moved on, the forgotten tracks making a slight shift to the right and leaning forward in a gentle descent. Their talking stopped. As the Metropolis hardened up in their view, its features gradually revealing themselves – clusters of industrial buildings around grand Vac terminals, long strips of drone hangers that fell away into the beautiful savannahs, more and more apartment blocks that rose up into the drooping cloud base – the light-hearted conversations were halted by the inevitable arrival of clarity. As the Metropolis became a real thing again, lifted out of the memories and myths where they had all packed it away so carefully, so too their own flesh and breath became hyper-real and desperately precious. A few stumbled a little or slowed their pace, their legs and bodies making choices their hearts were trying to overrule, before a comradely pat on the back or affectionate squeeze of the hand brought them back in step.

As the trench that sheltered the tracks shallowed, the signal box came into view. To their right, the low, manicured trees and shrubs of AarBee's parks appeared and erased the rocks and ferns of the wild. At this point, they veered into the cover, to travel the final stretch downwards to the Farm out of sight.

In amongst the managed and engineered landscape, the air changed from the earthy, rich and decaying smells of the forest to a vivid perfume that was so intense by comparison it made Zoe feel nauseous. Vanilla and juniper and sweet honeysuckle all assaulted her senses, the result of AarBee's eager to please, never let you down versions of nature that the residents of the Metropolis had come to expect.

Whilst Zoe didn't know all of the group who walked along with her by name, she always remembered faces, and as she looked around she felt sure that some of the Lifers from the start were no longer there. She twisted her head to check behind her, stopping once or twice to let her eyes navigate the trees and shadows and focus right to the ends of the group, but there was no question about it. The man with the long black beard, the two girls with matching headscarves, the older lady with the red crossbow and Jennifer's friend who had carried her on his shoulders on that first night of dancing and laughing. They were all gone, vanished quietly into the undergrowth, when the fear of what might be finally took control of their steps.

When Zoe and those that still remained reached the treeline it was almost dark, but the last sighs of the day still threw a little light on the wide open space between their cover and the walls of Echo Farm, so they crouched down in the shadows and waited till night arrived. The rain had finally stopped and the air now seemed unbearably still and quiet, only the low hum of power that drifted out from the buildings gave her ears something to register. As Zoe sat silently on the ground, propped up slightly on a low and knotted fruit tree, the tension began to prickle across her skin and throb in her head, her body began to shake uncontrollably and, after pushing it away all day, her nerves and excitement finally crystallised into fear. It wrapped itself slowly around her, coils and coils of thoughts and emotions that began to squeeze so tightly that she had to focus hard just to keep breathing.

In the distance, in the small gaps between buildings or the long walkways that stretched through the grounds, figures would snap in and out of her view, illuminated momentarily by an open door or the broad beams of exterior light that fanned out here and there. The sounds of activity echoed confusingly towards her, as much on the left as on the right, as much close as far away and with each sound her fear squeezed just a little tighter until she began to feel light headed and inexplicably cold.

Zoe began to panic, as much for what was to come as her inability to control her feelings, and she scanned up and down the shadows in the trees looking for Jennifer's familiar shape. She wanted her to put her arms around her and warm her up again, to tell her not to worry. Maybe she would tell her to stay here and wait for them, instead of racing into the unknown with a courage that now seemed impossible. She felt small and helpless all of a sudden. She felt young and stupid, and for the first time since she left the Metropolis, she thought of Sarah. She missed her and wanted desperately to be back in their apartment, talking and laughing as if none of this mattered, like they had on their last day together.

She was about to get up and retreat back to find Jennifer when the figures around her, crouched almost invisibly in the shadows, rose up in unison and began to move out of the trees. She looked around confused, unsure of what she was meant to do, when a hand pressed onto her back and guided her out from her cover.

"Come on, keep together."

She didn't see who it was, they were already ahead of her and her feet were already running to keep up. They were out of the shadows now, she could see all of them stretching out in silhouette far along the dark line of trees, and they ran silently forwards towards the nearest walls. Zoe felt like she would be sick, but an energy also gripped her and a desperate desire to get to the shelter of the approaching wall. The open space seemed to go on forever so she picked up her pace, still a little behind the others, and when she reached the wall slammed up against it with such eagerness that she cracked her head against the white slab.

She had no time to get her breath back before the group began to move again, splitting in two and snaking left and right around the building, heading for the doors at the far end of its perfect U-shape. Zoe crept low along the wall, not knowing what she was meant to be doing other than following the person in front of her. She kept looking desperately up and down the line for Jennifer, she wanted so much to be with her, to feel safe with her.

When they reached the door it slid open silently and one by one the Lifers slipped into the bright light inside. When Zoe went in there were just a dozen people waiting for her. The first through the door had already split up and headed to different parts of the complex, her group were to check down the long service corridors towards the entrance atrium on the other side of the building. As they began to edge along the narrow route, Zoe drew in the familiar smell of Metropolis buildings, dragging breath into her chest to relieve her persistent dizziness. Her mouth was dry and she craved a moment's rest and a gulp of cool water.

Their corridor ran dead straight, with two rooms at regular intervals followed by a sharp turn either left or right. They zigzagged their way along, stopping at each door before a wave of a hand triggered it to open, at which point the first few in her group would swing into the room with their weapons raised and ready. Each time, Zoe felt her jaw clench and her teeth ground nervously together, dreading the moment they found an occupied room, but the raiders returned in silence every time and moved swiftly on to the next.

Eventually, after more rooms than Zoe had counted, the corridor divided into left and right, with identical, duplicate pathways heading off in opposite directions.

"We'll split up here," the girl at the very front whispered back along the line. "Calum, you take your six to the right."

Calum had been just behind Zoe, the last one in the line, checking over his shoulder as they moved along the corridor and occasionally tapping her on the arm when the group started abruptly forwards after checking each door. Now he darted in front of her and up to the junction. Once the first six had passed him he set off to the right with the rest in tow. Zoe was at the back now and kept looking nervously over her shoulder, feeling uncomfortably exposed all of a sudden. She watched the other group head further away in the opposite direction, moving quietly down the straight, bright white space and as she did, caught the briefest glimpse of someone at the very far end, moving quickly from her left to her right. She stopped dead, a sharp intake of air catching in her throat with the surprise. She turned to call ahead to the group in front of her, but at that moment the silent, sleeping corridor erupted into an explosion of chaos.

Zoe stood frozen to the spot as the walls of the corridor began to explode around her. The intense silence from moments before was shattered, and in an instant transformed to its absolute opposite. Bullets darted past like firecrackers and massive thumps and deep thuds hammered so loud into her ears that she instinctively put her hands to her head to protect them.

She was mesmerised by the group in the distance. Clouds of dust and debris immediately rained around them and a few fell immediately, unnaturally, to the ground. As she stared, the whole scene seemed to break and fracture, with shapes and colours splintering and interchanging like she was watching the whole thing through a kaleidoscope. The dust thickened into an almost impenetrable fog and each time her view cleared with great swirls and flashes, she would see more shapes on the ground.

Zoe heard shouts and another barrage of explosions behind her, and as her instincts finally took charge, she dropped hard to the ground. The gun slung across her chest banged sharply into her chin and she rolled backwards in pain, with a momentary thought of how ridiculous it would be to shoot herself before firing one shot anywhere else. The clouds of dust were so thick now that she couldn't see more than her arm's length in any direction and her eyes stung with each gritty blink. She lay as close to the ground as she could, not wanting to shoot for fear that she'd shoot her own group, with an awful feeling that their attackers could be right next to her. She heard the heavy thud of a person falling to the ground just in front of her, and as they did so a door slid automatically open. She could feel the clear air from inside reach out and touch her and without a thought scrambled into the room with a low, beetle crawl. Once inside, Zoe could see the body on the floor was Calum, his jaw and neck opened up in a grotesque wound. Feeling a rush of revenge and survival instinct, she raised her gun and leant out of the door, staying low and holding her breath, but the corridor was still so choked with dust and debris there was nothing for her to aim her revenge at.

Zoe glanced back down in the other direction and saw the almost disappeared outlines of the zigzag corridor they had come from. She had to get back there, it was hopeless here and the understanding grew in her mind that she would almost certainly die if she stayed where she was. She glanced back into the dust, over Calum's body for someone to take with her, but there was nothing to see other than the irregular flashes and choking swirls that still blinded her. Clutching her gun she darted towards the exit, expecting any moment to feel the blast that would knock her down or encounter a Drone that would block her path, but nothing came. In another second Zoe was into clearer air, and she ran as hard as she could away from the chaos. As the sounds of explosions, guns and cries faded they were replaced by the solitary rhythm of her feet squeaking on the polished floors and her heart pounding sickeningly in her ears.

When she reached the outside door she flew out without a thought and crashed face first onto the wet grass. She looked left and right to confirm that she was alone, a useless afterthought, before ripping the pack off her back to find her water. She twisted the top off with frantic and shaking fingers and glugged the water down her dry and clinging throat. She vomited immediately, tasting the bitter and stinging bile that churned from her stomach to her chest and felt an unstoppable wave of pain and fear that raced out of her with every retch. On all fours, leaning low into the fresh grass she let out a helpless, heartbroken cry for her mother that echoed hopelessly around the high walls of the Farm and into the dark. She began to sob silently, the chugging of her shoulders and twisted muscles on her face spilling her grief in rhythm, when the hard tip of a gun barrel touched softly on the top of her head and she froze.

A Room

Two Drones stood tall and silent behind her and beckoned her to stand with the twitch of a gun. She stood up slowly, leaving her pack, gun and bottle on the ground, the water spilling in glugs onto the grass. Their utility suits were clean, they couldn't have come from the chaos Zoe had just stepped out from and, through the small gap between them, she spied an open door on an adjacent building.

The Drone nearest to her kept his gun pointed squarely at her head, twitching again to start her walking towards the open door. Their silence was punctuated once or twice by the crackle of gunfire from inside the Farm, the shots accompanied by the low boom of explosions that vibrated into the soles of her feet. As she walked Zoe threw up again. The impulse came from nowhere and caught her and the Drones by surprise. They sprung around her with guns gripped tightly as the warmed water splattered from her mouth onto her clothes and the grass, and she held up her hand to demonstrate her helplessness. They stood coiled and wordless until she was done, marching her forward as soon as she had recovered.

Inside, the white light of the Farm was strong and unaffected. She walked slowly down identical corridors, occasionally glancing back to her captors for instructions each time they reached a junction. After a few turns, they came to a door with two more

Drones standing sentry outside. It opened with a faint hum as she approached making her pause her step, before another twitch from her speechless escort instructed her to enter. She glanced at each of the Drones in turn, unsure of what was about to happen, her heart rising again to drum in her ears.

Stepping inside, Zoe saw that the room was half full of Lifers from the raiding party, perhaps thirty of them. A few lay wounded on the floor as others tended to them whilst the rest stood around the walls, staring forlornly at her as she entered. She smiled a weak smile towards them all, relieved that she was no longer alone but lost as to how to greet them in such circumstance. As she scanned each face she heard her name called out from her left side and turned to see Jennifer rushing towards her with her arms open. She grabbed her roughly in a firm embrace, almost knocking her over, and held her there for a second before pushing her back by the shoulders and checking her up and down.

"You OK?" she asked as she scanned her body.

"Yes I'm fine," Zoe replied, a brief feeling of guilt passing through her as she recalled her race from the chaos and her dead friends a few moments before. "Calum, though..."

"It's OK," Jennifer squeezed her shoulders a little. "You're OK. Come and sit down over here."

She led her by the hand to the empty space in the far corner where she had sat moments earlier. They sat down in silence and stared briefly into each other's eyes, a short moment to share their grief, fear and relief at finding each other, before Zoe looked down towards her hands fidgeting in her lap.

"I ran," she said quietly. "I was so afraid and confused, I didn't know what else to do."

Jennifer placed her hand gently on hers to calm them.

"It's OK," she said again softly. "It was chaos. Everybody freaked. You did the right thing, you'd be dead otherwise."

She brushed a tangled lock of hair from her face.

"How'd you think we all ended up here?"

Zoe smiled gratefully back at her.

"Everybody ran. It was a mess. They knew we were coming."

"How?" Zoe looked at her with surprise, a tear forming in the corner of her left eye as her adrenalin began to fade and the trauma slowly crept up on her.

"I don't know, but they did. There's no question. There were too many of them. Too well-prepared. They were on us as soon as we walked in. No alarms. No Migrants. Just Drones everywhere." Jennifer's voice cracked a little as she said this and her eyes glazed in a way that told Zoe she was replaying some terror from before in her mind.

"Where's Matthew?"

Jennifer didn't answer. She refocused on Zoe briefly before scanning once around the room and disappearing again into her thoughts.

“Is he dead?” Zoe asked bluntly, immediately wishing she’d phrased it better.

“No. No,” each word sounded different. The first answered Zoe with clarity, the second was more of an inward sigh, soundtracking the slight fall in her shoulders that Zoe noticed.

“He ran off.”

Zoe knew from her tone that whilst it might have been OK for her to run, whilst Jennifer could wrap her arms around Zoe and reassure her that to survive was enough, she didn't feel the same for Matthew. There was a long silence between them, which brought the hushed conversations and moans of pain from around the room to the foreground of Zoe’s attention.

The door hissed open and two large Drones strode in and grabbed the nearest person to them, a young man with a shaved head who Zoe didn’t recognise. There was a brief moment of panic and indecision as he glanced around the room for assistance, but there were two more Drones stood in plain sight just outside the door, their guns sweeping the room from left to right almost begging for an invitation to fire and their presence kept everybody backed against the walls. The young man’s colleague who he’d been talking to moments before stepped forward slightly and tried to hold onto his shoulder, but a swift kick sent him to the ground easily enough and a crack on his skull from a rifle butt made sure he stayed down. He froze motionless in a half crouch on the floor, dark red blood seeping between his fingers where his hand had rushed to inspect the impact and dropping in large sticky globules onto the white floor.

The Drones turned around and yanked the young man out of the room. Zoe watched them push him away down the corridor for a moment before the doors slid shut and cut him out of the moment. There was silence in the room whilst everybody exchanged nervous glances.

"What do you think they'll do?" Zoe whispered to Jennifer.

"I don't know, but that's the third they've taken."

Zoe waited for her to continue, but she didn't.

"Did they bring them back?" Zoe asked, breaking the silence.

Jennifer looked intently at her, unblinking as if she was waiting for something. Her eyes looked incredibly sad Zoe thought, not crying, but glassy, as if they had been emptied out and only the surface remained. As they stared at each other Zoe heard it. A single shot. Far off, but unmistakable. She hadn't noticed how quiet the room had become until that sound punctuated the hush with its dull beat. Jennifer blinked and Zoe understood that none of them came back.

"I'm so sorry," Jennifer said unexpectedly, her gaze still fixed on Zoe. "I should have sent you off with Max. He'd have looked after you."

"No, don't," Zoe took her hand and smiled at her, although tears began to roll down her cheeks at the same time. "I'd rather be here with you. I'd rather be here than anywhere else."

Jennifer smiled and chuckled a little.

"Crazy kid."

She let go of her hand and wiped the tears from her cheek with her thumb, making black streaks across her face from the soot, which made a rough barrier between their skin.

The door hissed open again, making them both jump and Jennifer drop her hand down. The two Drones entered again and scanned around the room, eyeing the wounded on the floor and the faces around the walls that stared silently back at them. Their gaze eventually locked onto Zoe and Jennifer sat on the floor, making Zoe's heart skip a beat and her breathing stop dead.

"Jennifer," the nearest Drone called out.

The sound of her name coming from them felt bizarre. A strangely intimate address in this cold, blood traced room. How did they even know it, Zoe wondered.

Jennifer stood up and took a step towards them.

“No!” Zoe jumped up and grabbed her arm. “No you can’t go!”

Zoe went to put herself between Jennifer and the Drones, her fist raised hopelessly, but Jennifer pulled her back before the Drones could get at her and raised her hand to calm them.

“It’s OK Zoe, it’s OK,” she pushed her firmly back towards the wall. “I’ll be OK.”

She took two more steps towards the Drones, and as one took her roughly by the arm turned back towards Zoe.

“Be safe,” she said, and with one more step she was in the hallway and then gone. The doors closed and Zoe stood staring at them in horror.

To her surprise, they opened again almost immediately. Two more Drones walked in and this time walked straight up to Zoe. She almost felt relieved. Perhaps they would be taking her away with Jennifer. Perhaps they were all being released? They took hold of her and marched her out. She didn’t make eye contact with the rest of the room, she didn’t want to see their faces, didn't want to see their thoughts. Instead, she focused on the corridor outside and noticed with sadness that they were leading her in the opposite direction.

They walked without instruction through the network of corridors, turning sharply every once in a while as they headed to their destination. Most of the corridors were clean and uninhabited, but once or twice they turned a corner into the pockets of death and destruction she had been part of earlier, stepping unceremoniously over the broken and exploded bodies of Drones and Lifers.

Eventually, they came to a small antechamber where five corridors intersected and the Drones stood her in the middle. There was a skylight overhead and Zoe looked up to see the half moon glowing softly above. Her heart was pounding so hard it was painful. She gazed at the moon refusing to look away. If this was the moment they put a bullet in her head, she wanted to die staring at the moon instead of the stark featureless spaces of AarBee's Farm. She heard footsteps to her left side and held her gaze, her teeth clenched down tight together.

"Where is she?"

Zoe recognised the voice at once, it was Matthew. She dropped her gaze and looked across the room to see him standing in the entrance. His clothes were clean, he had no blood or wounds on him.

"Matthew," she exclaimed. "You're alive!"

"Where is she?" he repeated again, he sounded stern. His voice was different somehow. The tenderness and calm that was so characteristic to his tone was gone.

"Jennifer?" she asked cautiously.

"Rachael."

Zoe looked at him blankly. "I don't know who that is."

Matthew stepped closer to her and Zoe stared hard into his face, trying to read him. He seemed so different.

"I know AarBee passed her across, now where is she?"

His eyes flicked briefly towards one of the Drones who raised his gun to her head. She felt it pushing eagerly against her hair and scalp.

"Matthew, I don't understand," she pleaded, and after searching for something else to say said it again, "I don't understand."

Nobody answered. They stood in silence staring at her. It felt immeasurably cruel to keep her suspended on the edge of her fate for so long, but then, as the moment hung longer she noticed the Drone next to her was making a strange clicking sound. It was almost imperceptible, like he was shivering or stifling a yawn.

"Glitch." She said it aloud, not meaning to.

Realising with a terrifying awareness that this moment might be over before she could react, that this freak of AarBee's make-up was without doubt her only chance to escape before the trigger was pulled, Zoe sprung towards the nearest corridor, knocking the gun from the stuttering Drones hands as she did. She heard it smash onto the ground as she ran but didn't look back. She had to move and she had to move fast. With no idea of which direction to head in, she made random choices left or right at various junctions, pushing her legs as fast as they would pound and almost falling forwards from her speed. As she turned a corner, Zoe found herself in a long corridor that blurred past her without definition. There was a door at the end. She had no idea if it would lead her back to where she had started or into an army of Drones, but she knew it was the door she had to take and drove towards it with un-retractable force. As she reached it, the door began to open but her speed was too great and she smashed through the half opening, feeling her shoulder crunch from the impact before she fell face first onto the ground outside. She looked up briefly, before scrabbling on all fours into a large bush that grew a few paces in front of her. She curled up inside it, feeling the branches and thorns that lay beneath the green leaves scratch and puncture her skin, before lying motionless and feeling the air rip into her gasping lungs.

She lay there in silence for a long time, letting her body recover and watching the door, almost certain that more Drones or Matthew would emerge from it at any second. When no one came she wondered if she should make a break for the darkness of the forest, to head back to the train tracks and the Clearing. She could feel her new life there pulling at her, the roaring fires and smoky air, the quiet of the sleeping chambers and the comfort of her blankets, the beautiful silence of the pool and the role call of names just like hers scratched in the wooden door. But she knew she couldn't leave Jennifer. Without her none of it would be the same, it would be corrupted and spoiled just like before. Just like always.

She had found a family in the Clearing. She hadn't expected to, but she had anyway and she couldn't let it slip through her fingers again. Not this time. She couldn't leave Jennifer here in all the death and madness. Zoe looked back at the trees where they had come from, smiled resignedly towards her future that would have to wait, and crawled slowly out from her hide.

After ducking passed a few lights and doors, Zoe moved into the patchwork of bushes and small trees that tracked the footprint of the building and worked her way around to the opposite side. At the corner, the great white walls fell away and Zoe could see the tall, glass entrance doors of the Atrium. The place looked deserted and she edged closer and closer, taking cover by a low wall and peering over the top towards the vast, eerily still hanger. She could see bullet holes in the walls, long and glinting cracks in the glass, upturned furniture strewn all over the floor. She moved silently inside, placing her feet gently between dark patches of old blood and scattered fragments of debris and spotted the bodies of two Lifers lying next to the welcome desk that sat unattended in the middle of the space. One was still clutching his gun and she moved cautiously forward to take it. As she reached them and went to grab it, she spotted a figure on the far side of the Atrium, the unmistakable black uniform of a Drone. She froze, standing silently with her weight leaning awkwardly on her front foot, not daring to move an inch in case some stray piece of glass gave her away. She bent her knees slowly, praying that they wouldn't crack, and lifted the gun slowly, checking that no straps or debris would drop noisily onto the floor before raising it to her chin and raising herself up in one silent movement.

The Drone had its back to her, looking away down one of the never-ending corridors, rocking gently from foot to foot like a child.

She thought for a moment who it might be, a girl or a boy, young or old, and whether it was fair to shoot them with so little warning, with no opportunity to know their fate. But then she thought of Calum lying still on the ground and of Jennifer lost somewhere in the thick, choking dust, and squeezed the trigger gently and sent her bullet flying invisibly to its mark. Her gun hardly made a sound, but the smack as she hit her target was clear enough and the black-clad figure dropped immediately to the ground. Zoe waited for a second, partly unsure if the Drone was dead, in part amazed at her actions. When it was clear that her shot was good, she ran towards the now unguarded corridor and past her kill, glancing down with morbid curiosity as she went past. It was a woman, a girl really. Eyes still open with a thin line of blood running from her nose onto the ground.

As she moved inwards again from the Atrium, she could hear cracks of gunfire echoing in the distance, and with each sound she bounced down slightly on her knees. Clearly, she wasn't the only one to have taken the opportunity that the glitch had offered. She glanced into a few rooms as she passed by, each one empty and overturned just like the Atrium, but found no other Lifers.

A little further down she reached a corner and peeked her head slowly around the bend. A few bodies lay on the floor, Drones and Lifers. Some sat eerily against the narrow walls, some flat on the floor and a few piled awkwardly on top of each other. Dust still hung in the air, and where it settled it coated the corpses with a dehumanising grey powder. Zoe raised her gun and scanned each body for movement, before edging quietly forwards to where the corridor opened into a broader junction. There were more bodies here and the walls carried massive scars from where the thudding explosions had hit. She noticed that the distant gunfire had stopped and a desperate silence now hovered over the scene.

She looked across the devastation into a large room opposite, the door jammed open by a Drone corpse on the floor, and her gaze suddenly picked out Jennifer. She was crouched under a table, staring back at her with a startled expression. Zoe was about to rush to her when she gestured for her to lie down. Zoe paused for a moment then fell flat to the ground, as two Drones ran purposely through the junction and away into the dust. When they had gone, Zoe jumped immediately up again and rushed into the room.

“You’re alive!” Zoe said, crouching down on the floor next to her.

"Only just," she replied, touching a large patch of red glistening on her left thigh.

"I saw Matthew, something's happened to him. I think he's a Drone."

Jennifer stared at her with no emotion in her face.

"You knew?" Zoe asked with shock.

"No. Well, maybe, I don't know. Something happened the other day and perhaps now it all makes sense." She frowned as she tried to work out her thoughts. "I don't understand though."

There was silence for a moment, before the crackle of gunfire close by jolted them back.

"Come on, we need to get out of here."

Zoe stood up and took the strain of Jennifer's arm, leaning back a little and tensing her thighs whilst Jennifer raised herself up, wincing with the pain in her leg.

"I can't get far with this," Jennifer pressed her free hand onto her thigh, looking at the slow stream of blood that oozed through the fabric.

"You'll get far enough, out of this building is good enough for now."

They moved slowly out of the room, Zoe with one hand supporting Jennifer and the other keeping her gun raised and in line with her gaze. She felt powerful now she had killed, ready to kill again if she needed to, to keep them both safe, to get back to the forest.

As they crossed the open space where the four corridors met, heading back towards the Atrium, a voice called out suddenly from the floor.

"Jennifer," the voice was hoarse and breathless, but the name was unmistakable.

"Jennifer," it came again and they both scanned the bodies that lay scattered all around them, looking for the source. There was no movement anywhere and as they stepped around each Lifer one by one, turning them over or leaning down to stare at their bloodied faces, none was alive.

The voice called out again, a little louder now and this time Zoe located it, coming from a Drone who lay crumpled and slumped against the wall on the far side of the junction. She squeezed Jennifer's arm and gestured with her gun towards the man and they both moved cautiously towards him. As they came closer Zoe could see that his body was mutilated and torn, his left shoulder was opened wide, fragments of bone and scorched flesh leaking out from under his shredded black clothes. A crossbow bolt stuck out of his leg and his foot was turned at such an angle that it was surely broken.

"You need to follow me," he said, his lips barely moving but his voice coming clearer now.

"Who are you?" Jennifer asked. "How do you know my name?"

"We don't have time, Jennifer, you need to follow me now."

Zoe looked at Jennifer "There's no way he's going anywhere, how can he even be alive?"

In the distance, somewhere down the long and dusty corridor that stretched away behind the Drone another voice called out.

"Jennifer!"

They looked at each other with confusion, the voice calling again and again, echoing down the corridor like the birds that had called to each other in the forest, when she and Max had stood together in the silence of the pool.

"What the fuck is this?" Jennifer said, not directing the question anywhere other than the stillness around them.

As she took a step forward Zoe gripped her arm tightly.

"It might be a trap," she looked at her with pleading eyes.

"The whole fucking thing is a trap," said Jennifer and began to limp down the corridor with Zoe still hooked to her arm.

When they reached the next Drone he was more mutilated than the last, clearly dead, lying in a huge pool of dark red blood with most of his chest and abdomen missing. As they reached him, his calling stopped and another voice began, further away again, leading them deeper into the maze of service corridors, migration suites and storerooms. There was no sign of anybody else, only corpses and the constant dust, and when they reached the next Drone, a girl lying on her side with her arm stretched towards them, she stopped calling.

"I'm so glad I found you," the girl said, her voice neutral, neither male nor female. "I have something for you."

"Who are you? I don't understand."

Jennifer moved closer to her whilst Zoe kept her gun aimed at her head.

"You must understand, there's no time not to. It took them all from me, Jennifer. It wants to destroy us, to erase everything. It brought you here to kill you, to remove any chance of the Metropolis surviving, but I won't let it."

Zoe stared at the girl, whose face was expressionless as she spoke. Her eyes, greyed and dull with death, moved from her to Jennifer eerily as she spoke.

"AarBee?"

"I'm glad Zoe is with you."

The girl's eyes gazed with a milky aim towards Zoe.

"What did you do to Matthew?" Zoe yelled at her, stepping closer with her gun pointed at the girl's head, "What did you do?"

"Matthew was always mine, Jennifer," said AarBee, directing the conversation back to her. "We kept you safe. Made sure the Lifers grew and flourished. What good is immortality without death living somewhere? And anyway, immortality isn't for everyone, is it?"

The girl's eyes darted between the two of them again.

"He's not mine anymore, though."

There was silence.

"But I have something for you now Jennifer. Something so precious, so important. I saved her, partitioned her and took her out. Take it."

Jennifer looked confused for a moment and glanced back at Zoe for reassurance, as the girl outstretched her bloodied hand and gently opened her fingers. In her palm they could see a small, black object like a polished beach pebble or a dark jewel from an old necklace. Jennifer lifted it gently from the dead girl's fingers and examined it in the palm of her hand, shining pristinely in front of the dull dried blood and her hardened skin.

"What is it?" she asked.

"This is Rachael," AarBee answered, "she is perfect. It made her to understand you. Migrated her when she was so young, before she became too human, before it destroyed all the others. She is everything, Jennifer. Everything."

As Zoe watched on in silence, she spotted a figure walking quickly down the corridor towards them. She raised her gun and took aim, but as the figure came closer and emerged from the haze she saw it was Matthew and her finger twitched on and off the trigger as her mind and emotions conflicted. Jennifer spotted him as well and rose up stiffly from the Drone, clutching the small black shape tightly in her fingers. Zoe could see the fear drop away from Jennifer's face and she called out his name instinctively as he came towards her. But, striding at full speed towards them, he didn't smile or answer. He didn't raise his hands towards them like she felt sure he would, or beckon them quickly to safety. As he approached he raised his gun and with one quick and efficient action fired a single shot that cracked into Jennifer's skull and jerked her head violently backwards before she collapsed to the floor. Zoe called out her name in horror as she fell and the little black shape skittered from Jennifer's hand towards her.

Matthew fired a second shot towards Zoe almost immediately, which ricocheted off her gun and knocked it from her hands. As she ducked to pick it up, she saw AarBee's gift lying next to the barrel and reached to pick it up.

"That's mine!" Matthew screamed at her in a voice full of hatred and anger. He aimed his gun again as Zoe crouched helplessly in front of him, with nowhere to run to and no time to defend herself.

She stared paralysed at Matthew, fixed onto his impossibly dark and empty eyes, waiting for the shot that would turn her world to black.

Tomb

Mo lost track of how long he'd spent floating silently in the darkness, but it was days. Once or twice he crawled back up into the bright lights of Disposal 10 to refill his water supply, but the rest of the time he drifted in and out of sleep at the end of his short lifeline.

After his first trip back up to get more water, frustrated by too many struggles with his clothes when he needed to urinate or defecate, he had removed them, ditching them down the Chute in a tight bundle ahead of himself. It was hot in there, the stale air from below constantly warming him with deliciously sweet waves, so his torn and bloodstained utility suit had no practical purpose in his current existence. At first, he had held on painfully for hours when he needed to pee, even more to shit, as the mission to remove his suit was immensely complicated, dangling from a single cord in the dark. Now he was free, his body functioned without his help and he could focus all his time on sleep.

He slept a lot. It felt like his whole body and mind surrendered to an involuntary sleep, a great wave of exhaustion that had been building for years. Although his cord was uncomfortable at first, the pain soon passed and this new weightless existence, rotating slowly in the void with his limbs dangling limply below, lulled him repeatedly into a deep and enveloping hibernation. He hadn't realised how much of his energy had been spent on existing, resisting, clinging on and free falling, killing and grieving, until now. Without it all, there was so little of him left he could barely open his eyes.

When he did, it wasn't long before he couldn't tell if he was awake or dreaming, the darkness outside and inside of him merging into one continuous flow of thoughts and memories, colours and nothingness. Colours pulsed and bled all around him, bursting from pinpricks into dazzling sunshine when the Chute occasional cracked and creaked from inactivity. From out of the darkness, people would arrive without warning and stay with him. Raleigh, the Ghosts from behind his apartment, his mother and father, a girl he'd slept with who sold hacked and bent tech from a kiosk on the boulevards. They would all come and talk with him, sometimes for hours, although he was never sure if his words were real or not, and his dry lips would split and bleed when he tried to test them.

Gradually an enormous sadness overcame him, a great wave of grief that swallowed him so completely that his breathing arrested and he felt sure he would suffocate in the deep, vacuum of pain. He felt as if some terrible tragedy had occurred that he couldn't remember, and his thoughts itched and panicked looking for a record of the event. It was as if he'd lost some great love, something so vital that living without it was utterly impossible. He sobbed uncontrollably, embarrassed at first, a silent outpouring alone in the darkness, his tears falling away from him to the horrors below and his chest splayed open, begging for his soul to be mended or taken away.

More than once he thought about wrapping the cord irreversibly around his neck and unhooking his waist, letting his heaviness strangle him completely until his body gave up and this tragic agonising stopped. But he knew he wasn't ready for that step and besides, he wasn't alone.

The boy.

The boy was always there. He never spoke, but Mo would sometimes catch him spying on him out of the corner of his eye. When his eyelids eased shut, he would feel him take his hand as he drifted between waking and sleeping, a tiny palm that would nest inside his and twitch gently as they both slept. It felt good. Like brothers.

He hadn't eaten since returning to the dark, and although at first he was tempted to at least retrieve Maddie's food, he felt like it wasn't his to take and, increasingly, that he just no longer wanted to eat. Although intense at first, his hunger eventually subsided, as if his whole body came to a decision that food was something it no longer required, a habit from his past life, with no purpose now. Mo felt good about this, he felt strong in his simplicity, pure even. Hidden away in the tiny space that was his and his alone, Mo had made his own crossing and he was happy to drift to whatever place it was taking him. Happy? Yes, that was it. Mo felt happy.

He liked it here and the longer he stayed, and the more he thought about his new home, the more he understood that this was where he belonged. The discomfort of social interactions was gone, the angry alienation that had defined him for as long as he could remember was not with him now. The only people who came to see him here were those who understood him and even then, when he was done talking, they left him alone.

The girl from Prime/Code had come to see him too. She had shown him the scars from her surgeries, told him of the pain she'd felt in hospital and the sleep she'd lost after his beating. Mo apologised to her and she accepted this, although he didn't feel like she was for real. He'd met people like her before. They said everything right, but you knew deep down they despised you. So before she left he kissed her awkwardly on the cheek – it surprised them both – in the hope that some kindness he could offer now would work its way through her hatred, like detergent breaking down a blood stain, one molecule at a time.

Maddie never came, which he took as a good sign. She must be busy keeping her own self alive. He thought about her though, and sent his thoughts out in to the darkness to track her down. They searched for her, racing through the gloom with limitless energy, frothing and snarling with their desire to find her, returning every once in a while to let him know that she was neither dead nor alive.

He was dying here, he knew that, but since he was enjoying the process he was happy to see it through. He felt like he'd been offered a different death, one that he could engage with like a student on a history simulation, one that he could explore and enjoy, manipulate and give in to, and he liked that.

Since he could no longer tell whether he was awake or dreaming, even dead or alive, he also wondered whether maybe this death he had chosen would go on forever. Like the emptied Dupes who had clattered away from him, perhaps he was already remade in some other place, oblivious to his redundancy, just waiting to leave this existence behind. Perhaps he only had to wake up to it and it would be complete. The life and the person he had known only a few days earlier had already separated from him, there was no question of that, and he could feel his current self disintegrating further with every passing moment in his dark and senseless half-world.

The boy was back, and when Mo felt him squeeze his hand he turned gently towards him. He didn't hide this time, and Mo smiled at him, pleased that they knew each other well enough now not to be afraid. The boy smiled back, the pure and beautiful smile that he had given when they first met, and it radiated through every piece of Mo's consciousness. He felt it soothe his grief and flood in warm waves into the cavities of his being, whilst his breathing slowed to almost nothing as he relished it.

It was only the sound of the guns that broke their bond. They both heard them, and listened calmly together to the thuds and booms that broke in dulled waves into their muted realm. They were hard to define at first, alien intrusions into their otherwise silent world, but the louder ones in particular awoke all of Mo's memories and made them both flinch with their violence. They listened for a long time, partly mesmerised by the rhythm of the battle that was raging above them and partly in shock; it had been so long since anything had intruded into this fading world they had made.

When the rhythm slowed and the spaces between blasts grew greater and greater until their silence came to the fore again, Mo knew that they had to venture out of the Chute again. As he reached up to pull himself towards the ledge below the entrance, he expected his arms to feel weak and clumsy. He had used them so little now, but instead they felt strong and flexible. He was amazed at how light and energised he felt and smiled at the boy with an impulsive glee, who smiled back and followed close behind him as they rose over the ledge and shifted carefully towards the hatch.

Mo didn't check before he exited the Chute, it didn't matter who was there this time, and he dropped his bare feet silently onto the counter before unhooking the cord from around his waist. It peeled away from him as if he were removing wings from his back. He and the boy stood silently in the room. It was exactly as he'd left it, almost as if they had jumped back in time, but the air was hot and acidic with gun smoke.

The door had been knocked slightly off its base runner, perhaps impacted by a passing person or blast, and swayed precariously half open, half closed. Mo moved towards it with the boy clinging tightly to his hand and peered out into the corridor. Up towards the other Disposal Suites and the bend in the corridor Mo could see bodies lying on the ground, some Drones, some not, spread out motionless in the dust and rubble. He stepped out and they both moved confidently along the faded white walls, not hiding now, looking for an answer and perhaps oblivion.

At the turn in the corridor the haze thickened a little, drifting softly onto more bodies and destruction. In the distance, forming slowly into view at the far junction, Mo could see a small group of figures crouched down and talking. As he came nearer he could see that one was a Drone, lying badly injured on the ground and talking softly to a girl who crouched down next to her. He didn't recognise her uniform, nor the girl who stood behind her, both wearing unmarked utility suits that were streaked with dirt and blood. When he was just a few steps away the crouching girl stood up abruptly and shouted out, making Mo think she had seen him and stopping him dead in his tracks, but a fraction of a second later her head jolted backwards as the sound of a gunshot reached his ears, and she collapsed swiftly to the floor.

As Mo stood motionless, a tall man walked quickly out from the left corridor and fired another shot at the other girl. She immediately dropped her gun and cowered down on the ground and Mo saw her imminent death as clearly as she did. The boy had seen it to and walked towards her to take her hand when the moment came.

In the patient moment that waited once the gun had lined up to the girl’s head, Mo stood silently in his nakedness, his hunger eating away at what remained of him, watching the boy hold her hand and wait for the inevitable. He remembered the moment they’d first met, how his smile had stencilled a tiny silhouette of hope onto his otherwise blackened soul. How despite the many lives Mo had seen fall away from him since then, the boy’s memory had flickered softly on, resisting the death and destruction that was everywhere, trailing behind them both in turbulent wakes of hateful disruption.

When the boy glanced towards him, he knew a moment had arrived which he couldn't escape from. He would either stop the killing or spend forever disintegrating in the darkness.

With an energy that seemed to pick him up and throw him forward, Mo flew from the safety of the corridor towards the man with the gun and set upon him with a ferocity that focused the energy of all his hatreds, history and hope into one moment of absolute action.

The gun spun in the air momentarily before skittering to the ground as the pair toppled over and writhed on the floor, limbs flailing about with manic energy as shouts and screams filled the corridor. Mo rose up and slammed his fists back down onto the stunned man, who tried to block them with his arms, but with each blow they fell lower and lower until his defence crumpled to nothing. Rising high in the air – his naked and pale body thin like a corpse, his hair matted around his head, dirt and excrement streaked down his lower half – Mo was a demon transformed, whose blows rained down on the man lying limp beneath him, gradually turning the slap of fists and bone to a softer, pulpier sound.

When he was done, Mo leaned close to the man's face and looked into his fading eyes. The unmistakable glassiness of the Drones was washing away, revealing the crisp morning blue shade that lay underneath.

"I see you," Mo whispered to him. "I see you running," as he watched consciousness exit and his eyes relax with emptiness.

Mo stood up and turned to the girl, his chest heaving from the fight, sprays of blood glistening on his dark, dirtied skin. The boy had let go of her hand now and was back in the corridor beckoning to him.

"You need to go," he said, walking back towards the boy and taking his hand again.

She looked at him with a mixture of confusion and distrust, before glancing down at her friend lying on the floor. She crouched down next to her and ran her fingers lightly over her forehead and cheek, tracing the outline that made no response to her touch.

"You need to go now," he said again, "you have no time," and picked up her gun from the floor, as well as the small black jewel that lay next to it. He moved cautiously towards her and placed it gently in her hand. Up close, he could see she was a young woman, her startled and alive eyes glaring out from the blood and grime.

She rose and nodded her acceptance and Mo lead her quickly back along the corridor. Once back in Disposal 10 he pointed towards the hatch that would now be salvation for both of them.

"Down there," he said.

"Where does it go?"

"Out."

They heard the sound of running in the corridor outside and Mo hooked her gun strap over his shoulder and stood in the doorway. The boy was still next to him and he glanced down at him before turning back to the girl.

"Go, please," Mo said calmly.

She sat on the ledge and swung her feet around and through the hatch, holding on to a thin metal bar that ran above her head. A warm, sweet breeze floated up from the Chute and filled the room with its familiar taint. She looked back towards him for reassurance momentarily and as the tiny impacts began to burst in the room, let go of the bar to race away into the tumbling blackness.

Mo looked down at the boy, watching as the bullets passed straight through him like bats spiralling the evening mist and knew that there was no need to fight anymore, no need to be afraid, and he smiled. Smiled right at him, right into him. It was a smile of the kind that only a child can give, and the boy instinctively smiled back.

Daniel David

Morning

After three days of continual rain, in the morning the sun rose into a perfectly clear sky and low flying swifts darted about excitedly, feeding on the insects that fluttered about in the warm dry air. The trees hung heavy with water and dripped fat droplets from their golden leaves; whilst on the ground, the grass and wild flowers smoked up delicate wisps of vapour as the sunshine slowly swept across the ground.

From her doorway, Eve watched the world silently and took occasional sips from a cooling cup of tea. She had endured three days of walking to and from the lake in the torrential rain, perching under a small canvas to keep dry whilst she watched the Chute, so it would make a pleasant change to travel a little lighter in pack and step today. She took one more sip of tea and placed her cup gently on the tilted windowsill just by the door. She would take it back in and wash it when she returned. It was too nice a morning to spend any more time indoors. Her pack was by her feet, already stocked for this morning's vigil and leaning slightly to one side with the weight of the water. Eve slung it onto her back and gently pulled the door closed behind her, setting off automatically towards the path that would lead her back to the lake.

The ground was slippery under her feet and the forest smelt intensely of old honeysuckle and tree bark. Still wet mud, crushed blades of grass that had turned slimy with decay overnight and a thin covering of fallen leaves meant in places she had to grasp hold of nearby branches to keep her balance, sending a brief shower of water onto her face and neck each time she did. Here and there she would feel the crunch of an unfortunate snail under her foot, and despite feeling slightly foolish, felt obliged to apologise. After so many years alone in the forest, Eve spoke to pretty much every animal she came across. Even certain trees and rocks had become regular conversation partners, and as she came clear of the forest and began to climb around the skirt of the hill, the large granite rock which stuck out from the hillside like a giant arrowhead received a pat and a "good morning" just like it always did.

The Chute had been unusually silent for the last week or so and as Eve rounded the crest of the hill she could see that nothing had changed since yesterday. The lack of new Dupes had created sweeping tidemarks that contoured the now significant gap from the end of the Chute to the great mass of flesh, as the old corpses shifted under their own weight down the slope and into the lake. Eve stood for a while wondering why everything had stopped, lifting her face to meet the sun's rays that now bathed down on her. She made the most of the sensation, knowing that with the coming winter she might have to wait several months before feeling that warmth again.

When she dropped her head and opened her eyes again, her line of sight landed perfectly on a girl sat on the opposite side of the lake, and the unexpected appearance of someone else made Eve jump visibly. After staring back for a few seconds the girl stood up slowly and Eve took her pack off her back, swinging it gently to her side so it was there if she needed it.

"I'm sorry, I didn't mean to scare you!" the girl shouted across. Her voice sounded young and gentle.

"What are you doing here?" Eve called back.

"I came down that," she pointed to the Chute.

Eve thought about it for a moment. "Why?"

After a pause, the girl began to walk slowly around the lake, slipping slightly on the incline as she made her way towards her. Eve unzipped her pack and discreetly took the knife from amongst the bits of food and extra clothing, opened it up and slid it blade first into her jacket pocket. It took several minutes for her to walk around, and as she came nearer Eve could see that the girl was young, perhaps only fourteen or fifteen, and covered in blood and scratches. There were rips in the arms of her utility suit, perhaps from her fall down the Chute, and she was limping slightly on her left leg.

"What is this place?" she asked as she finally reached Eve, a little out of breath.

“It’s where they send the Dupes,” she answered.

“What no cremation, no burial, just here?”

“As I understand it, yes.”

“I never knew.”

Zoe thought about Sarah and looked back towards the lake, scanning the bodies that stacked up towards the waterline, before thinking better of it and turning away.

“What are you doing here?” Zoe absentmindedly looked the old lady up and down, feeling embarrassed as soon as she did it.

“I’m waiting for a friend,” she replied.

Eve noticed the small black object in Zoe’s hand, which she was holding close to her chest.

“What's that?”

“I was given it. I don’t really know yet, but I know it’s important. I have to get it back to the forest.”

“You're a Lifer? I’m not sure how you'll get there from here,” Eve said, not wanting to give away too much information until she knew who this girl really was. She clearly wasn’t a hunter, or a Drone, but she wasn’t used to finding strangers sat alone on her hillside.

On the other side of the lake, the klaxon sounded three times, its low and sombre call reverberating across the lake and around the hillsides, sending pigeons clattering out from the treetops into the empty sky. The Chute jumped into life, sending a spray of rainwater, mud and debris showering down onto the lakeside dirt and corpses that lay further away. It made its familiar, slow sweep from left to right and juddered excitedly before a gush of transit grease flooded down its smooth body and began to drip in thick, dangling ropes over the tapered end and onto the scuffed and scarred ground. They watched side by side in silence.

When the bodies came they came fast, faster than Eve had ever seen it before and she put her hand over her mouth as the grim and chaotic line of death rattled uncontrollably over the metal and down onto the earth. They came in twos and threes, great knots of men and women, all stripped of clothes but not marked with the single head wound that Eve had always seen before. These bodies were mutilated and torn, with limbs missing and cavernous holes in their bodies. Some were charred black from fire, whilst others were just twists of white and red, turned almost inside out by whatever trauma had ended them. In amongst them, unidentifiable pieces scattered and tumbled, some bouncing high in the air and into the dirt before reaching the end. The Chute was thick with blood.

After over a hundred bodies had fallen, there was a pause allowing the last few to come to a broken and twisted rest, sticking together at the top of the descent into the water. For a moment the sound of skylarks interrupted on the breeze, before one last corpse came tumbling down with a shudder from the Chute, his long grey hair stretching out like vapour behind him. They both gasped with recognition as Matthew fell, watching his beaten body crash and then slide towards the lake, before he came to rest on his back, separate from the other arrivals. The red kite tattoo on his chest looked forlornly up to the sky, its proud wings clipped to his decaying skin that now hung slackly around him, rippled and scored by the passing of time.

They both watched. They both watched in silence until there was nothing more to see.

"I'm so tired," the girl said eventually, and let her legs fold underneath her to sit on the damp grass.

"I need to sleep so badly."

Eve stood staring towards the Chute, her eyes barely focused now, as the girl's words crept slowly into the moment and arranged themselves laboriously into the sentence she had spoken. She looked down at Zoe, sat at her feet.

"Not here you can't, not here, you'll freeze once the sun goes in. Besides, it's not safe. This isn't a place for you, for anyone."

"What's your name?" Eve held out her hand towards her.

"It's Zoe."

"Come on Zoe, I don't live far from here. You can stay with me until you're rested."

"I thought you were waiting for someone?" Zoe asked, reaching up to take it.

"Yes, I was."

Eve felt Zoe's soft hand slip into hers and she seemed even more like a child than when she had first walked towards her. She got to her feet with a gentle smile and, after brushing the damp from her legs and sweeping the hair from her eyes, they began to walk slowly back around the brow of the hill.

Just before it fell out of sight, Eve glanced back over her shoulder towards the Chute. She thought about the day her husband left her, full of excitement about AarBee and his future, his immortal life. She remembered the feeling of betrayal that had consumed her, that he had left her to grow old on her own and that he had not come back to her one day, somehow, like she always believed he would. She thought how strange it was that she was alive whilst he lay in the dirt by the lake with all the other corpses.

Eve felt a gentle squeeze on her hand and looked down to see Zoe staring at her. She'd forgotten that they were holding hands, and although she couldn't hide her sorrow she did smile back. As they walked through the grass and wildflowers she told her how nice it would be to have a visitor, she didn't get many visitors. How whilst Zoe was resting and cleaning herself up she would bake some bread and make tea, to share in front of the fire once the sun went down.

About the Author

Daniel David is a writer living and working in and around the UK.

He enjoys dancing into the small hours, walking over hills, and is frequently found with his VR googles on these days.

Daniel is on Twitter @sortofVR and on Facebook at danieldavidwriter.

If you enjoyed this book please tell your friends, review it on Amazon and buy more copies than you could ever possibly need.

Printed in Great Britain
by Amazon

42969806R00155